Henry William Lucy

Gideon Fleyce

A novel. Part 2

Henry William Lucy

Gideon Fleyce
A novel. Part 2

ISBN/EAN: 9783337051433

Printed in Europe, USA, Canada, Australia, Japan

Cover: Foto ©Andreas Hilbeck / pixelio.de

More available books at **www.hansebooks.com**

BY

HENRY W. LUCY

IN THREE VOLUMES

VOL. II.

London

CHATTO & WINDUS, PICCADILLY

1883

CONTENTS

OF

THE SECOND VOLUME.

GIDEON FLEYCE.

CHAPTER XIX.

THE CANDIDATE'S ADDRESS.

THE company were duly assembled at four o'clock in the library at Castle Fleyce, a cosy room with a splendid view, but deriving its name chiefly from a bookcase where Hume's 'History of England,' 'The Decline and Fall of the Roman Empire,' 'History of Rome,' and a collection of Mr. Robertson's histories, handsomely appointed and never opened, gleamed in new bindings.

Gideon entered a few minutes late, a little paler than was his wont, and with a compression about the brow indicative of intense thought. It was no new thing for him to approach the consideration of his address to the free and independent electors of Saxton. He had for nearly a year thought it over day and night, and had secretly studied many flowers of literature of the same kind blooming in other gardens. He now had the whole cut and dried and stored in the loft of his memory. But he wished to stand well with the assembled company, and meant to throw off in impromptu fashion the sentences so carefully and laboriously conned, and of which, to tell the truth, he was not a little proud.

Moreover, he wished O'Brien to know, and that presumptuous young jackanapes Bailey to understand, that he knew a great deal more about politics than he was credited with. He had begun to read the newspapers of late, not the murders and robberies, and general assortment of police news, which had formerly been his mental pabulum, but the leading articles. From the study of earlier addresses to electors he discovered that the great thing was not to be too precise in your declarations on any particular question of the day. By uncompromising approval he might gain six votes, but at the same time he would alienate half a dozen.

He cared just as much for what he largely and conveniently called 'the Land Question,' as he understood it. That was not much; but he did very clearly perceive that if he took one side he would have the tenants with him and the landlords against him, whilst if he went on the other side he would certainly lose the tenants' votes and might not gain the land-lords'.

He wanted to have both, and flattered him-self that in the line he had taken in his address he would make a sweep all round.

'Now, Mr. Bailey,' he said, 'if you will be good enough to act as secretary on this im-portant occasion, we shall get along. Here's pens, ink, and paper, and there's a bottle of claret, which I hope it won't be thought bribery

and corruption if Mr. Tandy joins us in a glass ;
and the rest not being voters, may have two.'

' Have you turned over the address in your
mind ? ' O'Brien asked, coming to business.

' Well, I have thought of it a little, and
have jotted down one or two of the heads.
There's the Eastern Question ; we must say
something on that.'

' Certainly,' said O'Brien, ' but not much ;
people are tired of the Eastern Question.'

' You must say a few words by way of
introduction,' Mr. Tandy ventured to observe.

' Oh yes,' said Gideon, impatiently, ' that
will be all right.   Now, Mr. Bailey, if you are
ready, here goes,' and Gideon dropped his left
hand in the bosom of his waistcoat, and, taking
a firm hold of his notes, began :—

' " To the free and independent electors of
the borough of Saxton.   Gentlemen,—Parliament has dissolved, and it forthwith becomes
your duty to elect a member for the new
House.   It is mine to briefly embody, with the

plainness and sincerity to which you are entitled, my political convictions, that you may
apprehend the character and complexion of the
sentiments which govern me now, and would
assuredly influence my vote in the House of
Parliament." '

Gideon paused and looked round for
applause.

' That's a very fair start,' said O'Brien.

' Don't you think,' said Jack, tossing off a
second glass of claret, which set him ahead of
the company by a clear fifty per cent., ' that's a
rather unfortunate phrase about " apprehending
the complexion of the sentiments "? You can't
apprehend a complexion, you know.'

Gideon looked at Jack with a face that
flushed with anger.

' You can write it down, Mr. Bailey,' he
said, with the slightest approach to a snuffle in
his voice, ' and if you have any criticisms to
offer you can make them on the proof sheet.'

' Oh,' said Jack, with the easy affability

that always aggravated Gideon, 'very well. But I thought we were here to discuss the matter as we went on.'

' " With regard to the Eastern Question," ' Gideon declaimed, continuing his address without further notice of Jack's impertinence, ' " my sympathies are always and always have been with the subject races of the Porte, though I plainly own, gentlemen, that as a lover of heroism I cannot forbear some sympathy to the nation that has been vanquished after a splendid resistance. Yet no doubts of the sincerity of Russian diplomacy can prohibit an emotion of respect for a nation which at an enormous cost of blood and treasure has emancipated thousands of Christians from Turkish misrule, and practically obliterated an empire whose career throughout the whole of European history has been attended by the curses and lamentations of oppressed or invaded peoples. When the attitude of Russia grows obtrusively sinister to our country, I shall be willing to band with you, gentlemen, and with all Englishmen in concerting measures for the national safety." '

' I rather think,' said Gideon, ' that's managed pretty neatly, and the language, perhaps, is not inaptly chosen.'

' You mean,' said O'Brien, ' that you run with the Turk and hunt with the Russe ? '

' That's rather a fine picture of you, banded with Messrs. Goldfinch, Burnap, Firminger, and Griggs, concerting measures for the national safety if the attitude of Russia grows of too sinister a nature to our country,' said Jack.

Gideon looked sharply at the youth, whose eyes were gravely bent upon the manuscript before him. He was strongly inclined to think that the young cub was chaffing him ; but Jack was as grave as a judge, and there was no doubt the sentence was a fine one. Gideon was glad to see that the youth was capable of being touched by a worthy emotion, and was inclined to forgive him his earlier impertinence.

' I think that is all I need to say on foreign politics. Now we will go on again : " Gentlemen,—So much on this point, I claim your leave to say, adding only that human foresight plays but an insignificant part in this world of accidents. But, gentlemen, when I turn to your internal policy, a fresher and kindlier interest possesses me. Here, at least, we deal with the hopes and struggles of our own countrymen. I apprehend there is no measure which should go to improve in however small a degree the general condition of the people but would command my steadfast advocacy. An ever-increasing number of votes in favour of proposed measures of great domestic interest, such as the County Franchise, the Burials Bill, Marriage with a Deceased Wife's Sister, exhibits the growth of public opinion and the sure illumination of Liberal culture. There are measures awaiting Parliamentary acceptance which affect the happiness of millions, containing elements to humanise the austerities of our social code; and in favour of such measures I should cordially vote." That is not committing myself to too much, I think. What do you say, Miss Tandy?'

'I don't know much about it,' said Napper, 'but it seems to me that if there is a fault in the general style of the address, it is that as far as it has gone you don't seem to be saying anything at all. It is rather as if you were trying to walk on both sides of the road at the same time.'

'Thank you, Miss Tandy,' said Gideon, flushing as if she had paid him the highest possible compliment. 'You have exactly hit it. After that I go on with greater encouragement. Now there is the land question, a very ticklish subject, on which we must say something. (That is not the address, Mr. Bailey, please don't write that down. I give you a wave of the hand when you go on with the address.) Now then: "Measures affecting agricultural interests must always enlist my deepest and most careful attention. The agricultural interests of this division of the county are of special magnitude, and I hold that your representatives, whether sitting as Conservatives or as Liberals, fail in a paramount condition of the duty they owe their constituents if they neglect to make themselves intimately acquainted with the opinions and wishes of those who follow agricultural pursuits. In a special degree would I here refer to the farmer's interest in the land he occupies. I hold that after having spent large sums of money in procuring artificial manures and in cultivating the soil into a high condition of fruitfulness the farmer is absolutely entitled to the benefit of those advantages which his capital and labour have brought about; and the Land Question, therefore, would find a cordial advocate in me. At the same time I would not pledge myself to any legislation on this question that did not impartially weigh the landlord's claim and so adjust the balance of equal rights. And such equitable adjustment, I am satisfied, is obtainable by cautious inquiry and narrow consideration of the arguments advanced by both sides."'

'What do you mean by the Land Question finding a cordial advocate in you, Mr. Fleyce?' asked Napper. 'I suppose there are two sides to the question, and you don't say which is to have your advocacy.'

'Miss Tandy,' said Gideon, beaming with pleasure, 'you ought to be in Parliament yourself. I think I must drop into my address a pledge to vote for women's rights. Is there anything else of a definite nature, O'Brien, that I should notice?'

'I think with Miss Tandy,' said O'Brien, 'that you have not erred on the side of definiteness; but perhaps you are right.'

'"I am averse to precipitate reforms,"' Gideon continued, waving his hand in sign to Jack, '"which in uprooting the weeds very often tear away the flowers of national memories and institutions; and in this respect

I am content to follow humbly the example of
that Grand Old Man—need I say I mean
William Ewart Gladstone?—who has grown
Grey and Glorious in the service of our common
country, whom to name is to do honour to
myself as a member of the great party with
whom History shall imperishably associate him,
whose capacious mind knows accurately and
with exquisite English sympathy to disconnect
what is base from what is good, to disentangle
the parasite from the pillar whose beauty it
hides, and to infuse new elements of health and
strength into forms and conditions of our constitutional existence which Conservatives suffer
to decay into the corruption that germinates
those national sicknesses by which empires are
killed." '

'Beautiful!' cried Jack Bailey, raising his
eyes to the ceiling and stealing a glance at
Napper as he brought them down. 'Burke is
not a patch on that.'

'Another glass of claret, Mr. Bailey,' said

Gideon, pleased at the enthusiasm of the young man.

This was a favourite passage with him, and he was glad to find it appreciated even by supercilious youth.

'I thought of putting that last, but perhaps I had better wind up with some references to this part of the country. Now, Mr. Bailey: "I cannot claim to have been born your neighbour, to have had my infantile slumber soothed by the roaring surge that beats on your shingly coast, but I do claim feelings of love for your town and country, which could not be deeper if Saxton were my native soil. All my chief interests are centred on Saxton. I have built myself a humble home here, which I hope will associate me and mine with your ancient borough for all time to come."'

'He means to get married,' Jack muttered to himself.

'Have you got that, Mr. Bailey?'
'Yes, sir.'

' " To Saxton I am united by bonds as deep as gratitude can forge. It is my delight and happiness to linger among the glories of its scenery and to claim fellowship with its sons. It would be my pride, as it is my ambition to be, not so much the representative as the benefactor of Saxton. But if by your help, gentlemen, I am elected as your member, you will be qualifying me to fulfil many secretly cherished hopes of being known to my constituents as a man who never lost an opportunity to promote their dearest interests, and who desired no better tribute to his endeavours than to be remembered as one who was very faithful in his adherence to the highest forms of Liberal policy, and devoted to the welfare of those who made him the proud recipient of their confidence." '

' I think that last paragraph will touch them up. Don't you think so ? ' Gideon said, looking round at the company with kindling eyes.

' Yes,' O'Brien answered, moving the

claret jug from the neighbourhood of Jack Bailey, who he thought might presently be saying something rude. It will be appreciated by the 'Longshore men, and, indeed, by the tradespeople generally.'

'Now, we'll get this printed right off, and let it flame from every wall in the borough in the morning. Perhaps you'll see to that, Mr. Bailey. You can get back in time for dinner.'

Gideon's banqueting table had been set for five—himself at the head, Miss Tandy on his right hand, O'Brien on his left, and Jack Bailey and Mr. Tandy *vis-à-vis* at the lower end. But this arrangement was disturbed by Miss Tandy's discovery of imperative engagements at home. She would walk by herself, not wishing to take her father away from the company in which he would be happy enough.

Also she peremptorily declined Jack's escort, a decision which caused that young man much surprise. He and Napper were already great friends, and with the audacity of youth he missed no opportunity of cementing the friend-ship. He thought it would be very pleasant to walk down to the town with Miss Napper, and he was already thinking that some delay might arise in the delivery of the manuscript to the printer, seeing that they would walk slowly, and he would, of course, see Miss Tardy to her father's door.

But Napper nipped this in the bud, and saw Jack off the premises with a start of a quarter of an hour before she ventured out.

The fact is Napper was sick at heart, and wanted to get into the fresh air with none but herself for companion. No one of the company she had just left would understand her feelings, least of all Gideon, who thought he had deepened the favourable impression long ago created. Napper had been very quiet at the so-called consultation, not only wholly for the reason which had moved others to the same course, and which was to be found in the fact that Gideon had really not asked them for consultation but summoned them for applause.

She had begun to suspect that his political character was a sham, and this ornate saying of nothing in long words to the electors was final confirmatory evidence. She had expected to hear some brave, simple words addressed to the people on the questions of the day. Instead of which Gideon had turned his early education to account in an effort to say as little as possible regarding his convictions, if, indeed, he had any, and by all means not to offend the prejudices of others.

Napper had looked forward hopefully to the contest in the borough, where, as she understood, the electors had hitherto had no voice. But, she felt with pain, here was a sorry commencement.

CHAPTER XX.

'HOW THEY BROUGHT THE NEWS TO GHENT.'

NEWS travels slowly through the highways and byways of Saxton. Towards noon each day the carrier, coming in from the Junction, brought thirteen of the London daily papers, which he delivered at as many houses, being those of the intellectual aristocracy of the town. Whilst all Great Britain and Ireland were vibrating with the news flashed hither and thither by telegraph, and echoed by every tongue, that a dissolution of Parliament, long expected, had come when no one looked for it, Saxton slept on under the thin March sunlight,

> Rocked by breezes, touched by tender light,
> And sung to by the sea.

Down on the beach the 'Longshore men still stood at gaze, looking out over the tossed waters for the ship that never came home. They were exactly the same, save that they had put monkey jackets over their jerseys. With many of them this was evidently an empty compliment to the season and a deference to prejudice, for they wore the garment wide open at the chest, and the keen wind, salt-laden from the sea, beating about their bosoms, found them barricaded only by the familiar jersey. As in the heats of summer, so in depths of winter, their hands were far down in their capacious trousers pockets, that evidently being an attitude which long experience had suggested was best calculated to fit them for sudden emergencies such as befall on our English coasts.

All unconscious of the great news which Gideon had brought down from the Castle, they chewed the contemplative cud and fixed their eyes on the far horizon.

At the same hour on this memorable Tuesday, Mr. Goldfinch sat at the desk in his shop in High Street, whilst his young men bustled about making up pounds of sugar, brown and white loaf, weighing out ounces of tea, and deftly slicing pounds and half-pounds of butter from the great tub-shaped heap on the counter. Mr. Goldfinch sometimes lent a hand on a Saturday when the market people streamed in on their way homewards. But as a rule circumstances permitted him throughout the day to perch his little high-dried body on a stool behind a desk on the left-hand side just as you enter the shop.

Here he was supposed to be intent upon the making out of bills; but the position had other advantages. From this commanding height he could survey the shop and see that Pilcher combined the proper proportion of rapidity in making up the parcels with the suavity desirable when addressing ready-money customers, and that Philpot, who was getting a little shaky, did not

spill the tea on the floor when he took it out
ot the big canister.

Also Mr. Goldfinch was able to act as time-
keeper to Tom Prodgers, who went out with a
large basket distributing provisions throughout
the town like a good genius. This was a duty
at once engrossing and exciting. Prodgers,
sen., was a 'Longshore man, and perhaps it was
the taint of blood that led to the formation of
a habit on the part of Prodgers, jun., to set
down his basket in shady places and refresh
himself with a game at marbles, pitch-and-toss
for brass buttons, or whipping top, as the
season might be. In the winter he made
slides before the doors of the almshouses and
watched for the outcoming of unsuspecting
tenants, or engaged in deadly combat of snow-
balls with the doctor's lad and the red-faced
boy from Firminger's.

During the early weeks of his engagement
he had attempted to meet the reproaches of his
master with affirmation that he had been ' gone

only ten minutes,' or at most a quarter of an hour. But the ready production of Mr. Goldfinch's figures showed the hopelessness of this endeavour, and Tom was driven either to the invention of fabulous excuses for non-appearance in due time or to relapse into sullen obstinacy when confronted by proofs of his guilt.

Another thing which Mr. Goldfinch found desirable in connection with the post was that, being out of the way of interference with actual business it afforded him opportunities of chatting with customers as they passed out. Tuesday was not a very busy day, and the few customers that came were at leisure to discuss general affairs. If they had only known the intelligence which the world a few miles outside was throbbing with, what a day they would have had to be sure! As it was, the delight was deferred by some hours, and now they had no choicer topics for talk than the weather, the condition of trade, the newest burial, the latest death, and the wedding nearest in prospect.

Mr. Firminger was at this same hour quite alone in his shop. On Tuesdays the custom of the week began to revive, but only with languid breath. His stock had run very low, being chiefly composed of the leavings of Saturday night, and Mr. Firminger, with his blue apron aggressively tied on, was now engaged in rounding off stray bits of meat and trimming them to make them look as inviting as possible. This he did with great energy, using his knife almost viciously, as if he bore a personal grudge to the meat. But that was merely a habit of mind and had no personal application.

'He always came down straight on the block,' as he said, and when a piece of meat that lay thereon was thin he carried out this axiom literally, chopping off bits of hard wood after the blade had passed through the layer of meat.

Mr. Firminger always did things in that way, and was rather proud of it than otherwise.

'Plenty more where that comes from,' he

was accustomed to say, when the superfluous energy of his action was commented upon, and it was suggested that he might spare himself a bit.

If he attempted to drive a nail into the wall he generally either broke it off short or buried it up to the head with a sledge-hammer blow.   If on Sunday afternoon, going out with Mrs. Firminger, and the latest born in the perambulator, he essayed to propel the conveyance, he dealt with it as if it were a handcart. If he helped Mrs. Firminger into the dogcart, she usually found herself in imminent danger of falling out on the other side.   To this day she bears on her matronly bosom the mark of a pin which her spouse, in a well-meant effort to fasten her shawl, had driven an inch or two into her flesh.

If Mr. Firminger had heard of the good news from London it might have been supposed that, in his mind's eye, he had on his block the claims of the rival candidates, and that he was making mincemeat of them.   But, in truth, he knew nothing, and was only trimming a bit of mutton.

Mr. John Griggs, as becomes an upholsterer in a large way of business, did not sit in his shop, having an office at the back, where he received customers, and whence he was at all times willing to emerge to conduct them over his stock. Next to Mr. Burnap, who had had the building contract for Castle Fleyce, Mr. Griggs had up to now made the most out of the new candidate. As already recorded, he had had a commission for furnishing the place, and the transaction had left many bank notes sticking to his fingers.

He was more than ever convinced of the desirableness of the borough never again falling into the condition of affairs wherein a neighbouring landowner assumed as a right its Parliamentary representation and warned off all other candidates.

Mr. Griggs sat at his desk checking off an estimate, and from time to time applying a large blue pocket-handkerchief to a small pink nose. He had an exceedingly minute fire in a stove, which, if enclosed in one of the wardrobes in the shop outside, might have warmed its interior, but was wholly inadequate to the task in the office, more particularly as Mr. Griggs sat with the door open, holding the theory that to have it closed repelled possible customers. There were no windows to Mr. Firminger's establishment, which to all intents and purposes was an open stall. But the atmosphere there seemed much less chilly than in Mr. Griggs' shop with its faint smell of wood and varnish, and its partial illumination by the pinched nose of the austere proprietor.

Mr. Burnap was away on business in Lampborough, and was the first, outside of the inner circle gathered around Gideon, to hear the great news. Mr. Burnap was at first inclined to give up the errand which had taken him to town, and hasten back, lest peradventure some one should rob him of the distinction and delight of first telling Firminger and Griggs and Goldfinch. But on reflection he thought he might safely secure the profits of his business, and still retain the privilege of being the first to communicate the news. The papers did not often get in much before one o'clock. Neither Firminger, Griggs, nor Goldfinch took a paper, waiting till after business hours, when, at the Blue Lion, some one looked through the news of the day and read tid-bits out for the benefit of the company. Those who bought the papers would have to read them first; then they would surely wait to get their dinner (the hour for which in Saxton was one o'clock) before going out to spread the news.

Mr. Burnap thought he was safe up to two o'clock, but would take care not to be later than half-past one. News like this did not come every day, and opportunities were not to be trifled with.

At the same time, he could not afford to miss the bargain that had taken him to Lampborough. The fact was, an old church on the other side of the county was going to be 'restored.' The splendid oak pews, the wood of which was at least three hundred years old, were offered for sale amongst the other old materials. Burnap, who was not without occasional flashes of idea, had seen to what use this choice wood could be put. When doing up the Castle he had put in round the hall a bit of wainscoting a foot high. It was of oak, and well enough in its way; but these pew doors and front and back divisions would make quite unique wainscoting for the hall.

Burnap meant to glance over them with a deprecating eye, to throw out a hint that they might do for mending up old things, pick them up cheap, and re-sell them to Gideon at something over their real value, and that was considerable.

The sale was a little protracted, and though it began at ten o'clock in the morning, it was half-past twelve before the old pews were knocked down to Mr. Burnap at a remarkably reasonable figure. It was a ten-mile drive to Saxton, a distance already performed by Mr. Burnap's mare, who, in addition, was getting up in years. He could not hope to do the distance under an hour and a half, but then he would be in by two. So, sacrificing his dinner at the one o'clock ordinary, an institution on which he had cast a kindly thought when driving towards Lampborough in the morning, he had the mare put in, and drove at what she thought an unnecessarily hasty pace towards Saxton.

Two o'clock was striking as he drove along High Street, meaning to call first on Mr. Griggs, whose shop lay in the way. As he drew up at the door, whom should he see through the glass but Mr. Tandy talking to Griggs, who was nervously mopping his nose and betraying other signs of excitement which too surely disclosed the truth. When Mr. Griggs beheld Mr. Burnap muffled up to the chin, sitting in the trap at his door, he dashed past Mr. Tandy, to that gentleman's surprised discomfiture, and closed the door after him, to prevent his too early participation in conversation.

'Good morning, Burnap. Going out for a drive, I suppose? I've got some news that will make you warm.'

'Is it about the dissolution?' Mr. Burnap growled, feeling just cause for resentment. 'Oh, I heard that two or three hours ago, and was just thinking of looking in to tell you, but was too busy.'

Mr. Burnap felt he had Griggs there, the effect of his rapid repulse being the' greater owing to the lowness of the temperature, which gave the upholsterer a peculiarly miserable and depressed look.

'Have you heard this long, Mr. Tandy?' Mr. Burnap continued, as the solicitor delivered himself from his imprisonment and appeared on the doorstep.

It just flashed upon Mr. Burnap that this might have been the first place Mr. Tandy had visited, and that if he made haste he might still triumph over Goldfinch and Firminger.

'No,' said Mr. Tandy, 'only about a couple of hours. Mr. Fleyce had a telegram this morning from Captain O'Brien, and drove over to the Junction for the papers. I have just been round to our friends Goldfinch and Firminger to tell them we shall have the address to-night and must get to work forthwith. We mean to have a good stylish committee for conducting the election, but of course we'll have to do all the work, and must talk it over. I'm going up to the Castle at four o'clock to see about the address, and shall probably stop afterwards to have a snack. But I'll be down at the Blue Lion at half past eight, and we will discuss matters.'

Mr. Burnap, who was a short-tempered man, heard this explanation with mingled feelings. What business had Tandy to go bustling

about with a bit of news as if it were a hot
potato and burnt his fingers? It was a long
time since Mr. Burnap had had such a chance,
and now by this fellow's meddlesomeness he
had lost it.

'Tandy's no more nor a child,' he muttered, as he drove off. 'If he hears anything
he must go running all over the place to tell it.
I've no patience with such ways.'

Then, again, Mr. Burnap wished the actual
commencement of electioneering proceedings
had been delayed for whatever time was
necessary for him to dispose of the pews to
Gideon. At various consultations of the candidate with his friends since the first time they
met at the Blue Lion, Gideon had shown a
nervous apprehension of anything that would
bring him within the grasp of the law. He was
not going, as he plainly said, to spend a lot of
money on his election and find himself turned
out on petition because of some inconsiderate
action on the part of his agent.

That was 'all bosh,' as Mr. Firminger said. There was only one way of winning Saxton, and that would only have to be adopted. But it was well understood that Gideon, having convinced himself of the necessity of the old plan, would not stand in the way of its adoption. He would find whatever money was necessary. That was quite settled, though he insisted on knowing nothing of how the cash was disposed of, a stipulation which entirely met the views of Mr. Burnap, Mr. Firminger, Mr. Griggs, and Mr. Goldfinch.

But in the matter of the pews there might be a difference. The sale would be a personal transaction between himself and Gideon, and, as he did not mean to have his journey to Lampborough for nothing, he was not sure how far the bargain he intended to strike would meet with the approval of the election judges if they insisted upon inquiring into it.

On this head he received some assurance from Mr. Tandy, when they met at the Blue

Lion later in the evening. Mr. Burnap was careful not to go too minutely into particulars. In fact he led Mr. Tandy to believe that the bargain had already progressed some distance, and what he professed himself most anxious about was whether an ordinary business transaction between an honest builder and an enterprising houseowner would assume a criminal aspect, because of the imminence of an election in which both would take a prominent part?

He learned with satisfaction that as the writ was not yet issued, and that even a week or two must elapse before Parliament would be dissolved, there could not be any harm in proceeding with a business transaction of that kind.

Relieved on this head, and mollified by the present possession of a second glass of hot whisky and water, and the near prospect of an unlimited supply chargeable to ' the committee,' Mr. Burnap simmered down from the condition of asperity in which he had fallen when he discovered that Mr. Tandy had forestalled him with the news. He was even in high spirits, and by way of salutation laid his hand on Mr. Griggs' shoulder with a friendly cordiality which shook every bone in the upholsterer's body, and seemed to make his cold worse than ever.

The news variously affected the Conscript Fathers. Mr. Burnap was inclined to be boisterous. Mr. Griggs was exceedingly nervous, and already began to forecast lamentable defeat for the Liberal candidate. Mr. Goldfinch took on a certain air of serenity which grew more beautiful, as in honour of this occasion he ordered more than one extra tumbler. His disposition to go back to '32 and relate with minute detail what had taken place at that epoch became in time a little wearisome. Perhaps it was scarcely fair upon him that this narrative should have been persistently interrupted, generally by the not over-well-bred Burnap. It may be all very well to judge of Hercules by the measure of his foot. But it is not fair to a chronicler to snap him up before he is half way through his story, sometimes when he is barely on the threshold of it.

This was Goldfinch's fate, and it says a great deal for his natural good temper that he did not resent the interruption, but, the piping of his thin voice being drowned amid the thunder of a casual remark from Mr. Burnap, he subsided with a watery smile of resignation, watching for a fresh opportunity to narrate a story so curiously apposite.

Mr. Firminger, while not so fluent as Mr. Burnap, was quite as noisy, and very anxious for an opportunity of immediately 'coming down on the block.' Mr. Tandy was the quietest at the festive board, and the most seriously occupied with plans for conducting the campaign. Hitherto, though Gideon had dipped pretty deeply in his pocket, there had been nothing in the shape of a fund available for general expenses, nor had there been any authority given to him by Gideon to pledge his credit. However, Mr. Tandy had thought himself justified in ordering a private room at the Blue Lion which it was intended should be the headquarters of the Liberal committee.

As yet he thought it desirable that gentlemen should pay for their own refreshments, but probably on the morrow, when the address was actually out, it might seem appropriate that the labours of the committee, gratuitously rendered, should be lightened by judicious provision of meat and drink.

Mr. Tandy had brought in with him a proof of the address, wet from the press, and its meaning strangely darkened by eccentricities on the part of the printer, whose work had not yet been revised. It was fresh evidence of the great merit of this literary effort that it sounded quite as well with the printer's improvements as it had done when dictated by Gideon. It meant about as much now as it did then

But, meaning apart, there was a ring about

the phrases and a generous eloquence throughout which increased Mr. Burnap's respect for a
gentleman who had incurred a large building
account, and brought tears into the eyes of Mr.
Goldfinch when he recollected how in that very
room, fifty years ago, Mr. Montgomery, father
of the present Conservative candidate, now
dead, and buried in the churchyard, where the
tombstone had only a fortnight ago been re-
lettered owing to growing a little indefinite by
the weeds and the moss which got on it quite
unaccountably—had in that very room read an
address which he (Mr. Goldfinch) would not
say was more eloquent; but it certainly did
seem to him that in those days the gentlemen
who came forward as candidates were, on the
whole—he didn't say there were not exceptions
—but, on the whole, better than those of to-
day, and more good to the borough, more free
in their allowances of tea and coffee to the
servants, and less inquisitive about an extra
pound of sugar here and there in the week's bill.

CHAPTER XXI.

THE 'LONGSHORE MEN WAKE UP.

THE news spread the next morning with the light of the tardy sun. Like the sunlight it diffused warmth and brightness wherever it fell. Everybody, from the prosperous tradesmen in High Street to the fisherman's family in the back court behind the Dog and Duck, felt cheered by the intelligence.

As for the 'Longshore men, the news immediately distracted their attention from the horizon, and all their thoughts were turned landward within the boundaries of the borough. They set their hands deeper into their pockets with the sure and certain hope that presently those receptacles would contain something beyond their ordinary complement of bone and

flesh, a jack knife, a baccy box, and some odd
pieces of twine apparently stored there with
the expectation that they would be very useful
supposing a ship were driven ashore in a gale of
wind.   Also they chewed their quid of tobacco
with a profound and gentle comtemplation.

There had come to them the crisis in the
life of every free-born Englishman, being also a
householder.   Within a measurable distance of
time they would be called upon to exercise the
franchise.   There was not a man treading the
beach that did not feel his new responsibility,
whilst some turned over in the slow machinery
of their minds tales they had heard at the
family board of how some worthy sire at
earlier elections had managed not only to obtain
his due from the candidate for whom he voted,
but had done his party the further service of
taking a bribe from the opposite side, and so
had spoiled the Egyptians.

These were matters not to be disposed of
lightly, and the 'Longshore men were not a

community given to undue haste. Everything comes to the man who waits. They were accustomed to wait, and had no doubt that in due time both candidates would come to them.

It was curious that from the second day after Sir Stafford Northcote had announced the dissolution in the House, the publicans of Saxton began to prosper, whilst most other trades stood still. The 'Longshore men, exhausted with profound meditation on the beach, resorted a little earlier than usual to the Dog and Duck, and did not retire until the utmost limit of time permitted by the legislature. They had a good deal to talk about, and found that speech flowed easier, and that thought came quicker, when the mental machinery was oiled with rum and soothed with tobacco.

That Gideon was the favourite was clear from the first. He never showed himself in the streets but there gathered at his heels a crowd of small boys, who cheered incessantly. Prod-

gers, jun., was so demoralised by the excitement of the time that he absented himself for
the space of two hours on an errand that,
rigidly performed, would not have required
more than ten minutes. When he came back
Mr. Goldfinch placed a week's wages in his
hands and bade him go forth, which he did
joyfully. Being thus released from commercial
cares, he was able to devote all his spare time
to politics, and from the first associated himself
enthusiastically with the Liberal cause and its
champion in Saxton.

Gideon had not only with him the boys
of the borough, but their mothers, who, less
critical in their taste than some people, were
much taken by the newness of his clothes, a con-
quest confirmed by the affability of his manner.
Gideon missed no opportunity of upholding the
purity of election, and, as Mr. Burnap had
complained, was always insisting that the law
should be respected. At the same time, when
seated on rushbottomed chairs in the humble

homes of accessible electors, he had a way of looking pounds of tea and smiling Christmas joints that had a marvellous effect upon womankind, on whom the cares of the household pressed heavily. They knew he could not now make good these shadowy promises. But when he was elected and all was safe, then it was clear there would be no more open-handed and genial gentleman in the neighbourhood than the owner of Castle Fleyce.

From the children to the mothers up to the heads of the household, the transition of popularity was naturally and fully accomplished. As became their greater and more immediate interest, the free and independent electors were not to be bound by nods and winks and wreathed smiles. What they wanted to know was 'Is the 3*l.* right?'

From time immemorial the free and independent electors of Saxton had enjoyed their birthright of a minimum of 3*l.*, payable whenever a contested election took place. This is alluded to as a minimum because in addition to this sum, paid down on the nail before the free and independent went to the poll, there were contingent advantages in the shape of beer money, fees for watching, for putting up poles, and for doing various other acts of which the chief practical recommendation appeared to be that they made it possible to hand over a certain sum of money to the elector in the legal form of wages.

Beyond this there was also that ecstatic thought which had stirred the dull and murky waters of the minds of the 'Longshore men, and had pointed to the possibility of getting 3*l.* from both sides. Unfortunately no man had yet discovered means by which an honest elector could take wages from both sides, either as a watcher or a builder up of mighty poles. Such dual service must be inevitably detected. But since the ballot had come in there was no obstacle to the expansion of the patriotic duty of making two blades of grass (in the shape of receipt of 3*l.*) grow where previously only one had flourished. It was the first contested election that had taken place under the Ballot Act in Saxton, and its possible advantages in this direction uplifted the hearts of the electors.

Mr. Montgomery, the sitting member, had heard the dread news of the dissolution from his place in the House of Commons, and received it with as much geniality as might be expected of a man suddenly informed of an unexpected call upon him for 5,000*l.* Knowing something of the way in which 'this money-lending fellow' was conducting the contest, Mr. Montgomery had put down his own share of the expenses at that sum. At first he, like Captain O'Brien and Sir Henry Gilbert, had been inclined to undervalue Gideon's capacity. The notion of a vulgar interloper like this coming down to Saxton and disturbing in his family possession so worthy a person as Mr. Montgomery, had seemed the height of the ridiculous.

But as Gideon went on his dogged way, and, above all, as he showed his hand by leasing the old Castle, rebuilding it, and taking up his habitation there at a vast weekly expense, Mr. Montgomery began to open his eyes and to move uneasily in his chair. He did not doubt the ultimate issue. It was absurd to think that Saxton would reject a Montgomery for a 'money-lending fellow from London.' But there would be a fight. A fight meant money, and Mr. Montgomery hated to be called upon to dispense that article beyond the level proportion of annual contributions, which he paid as regularly and as cheerfully as he paid his taxes.

A little while ago, when the inevitable nearness of a general election had excited some of his friends in the House, he had looked on with an easy smile, and felt how nice it was to have a snug constituency all to himself and his family. But things were changed now, and this confounded ballot deepened the seriousness of the aspect. Formerly the free and independent electors disposed to make a change in their Parliamentary representation would have to take account of the pains and penalties of making an enemy of a rich and influential neighbour. Now they might vote as they pleased, without any one being the wiser, a state of things under which, Mr. Montgomery had it borne upon him, he would be the loser.

He was a model member, as members go in country places. He gave a guinea here and there to various local charities. He never went so far as to dine at the farmers' ordinary, but at agricultural shows and ploughing match dinners he sat at the head of the table, near the chairman, and when dinner was over he delivered, in a loud voice and without punctuation, some remarks that were the echo of the noisiest and most uncompromising speech delivered from the Conservative benches during the preceding session of Parliament.

He honestly believed all he said, just as in

the time before Galileo people believed the sun
went round the earth.   He never inquired into
the matter himself, and probably would not
have been much wiser if he had.   He was a
Tory as his father had been, and as his grandfather was.   He had no passion for politics, and
no particular desire for senatorial honours.   He
didn't like London in the season with its bustle,
its frivolity, and its expense, and would have
preferred to spend the summer months at the
Hall.   But a Montgomery had always been
member for Saxton, and he would as soon have
thought of giving up the family seat near
Saxton as of abandoning the family seat at
Westminster.

All the old apathy vanished at the sight of
opposition.   If even it had been some decent
man of eminence or respectability on the other
side who had come forward to tussle with him
for his birthright, Mr. Montgomery would have
felt less sore.   But the money-lending fellow,
with his smug face and new cloth s and his

uproarious popularity in the borough, was more than he could stand.

He came down to Saxton early on the morning after the announcement in the House. He was in the train earlier than O'Brien, for, being a country gentleman, he was accustomed, when the Whip permitted it, not only to go to bed early but to rise early. He had the family solicitor up at the hall, and the consultation which followed did not tend to reassure him. It was clear that Gideon meant business, and it was also beyond doubt that he had made some way in the race. That he should win was an idea Mr. Montgomery still scouted. But the contest would be an exciting and expensive one.

'What business does a fellow like that want here, Muffleton?' he said, turning upon the good solicitor a face that could scarcely have been angrier if he had suspected him of having a hand in bringing the interloper down. 'This is a respectable borough that has been in my family since the first Parliament of Queen Anne. Of course, we have had to fight it once or twice ; but for years there has been no sign of a contest, and now, just when things are dull, rents are down and hard to get in, and I have three farms on my hands, this money-lending fellow comes along, springing up out of the earth or gutter, heaven knows where.'

It was astonishing what comfort Mr. Montgomery derived from alluding to Gideon as ' that money-lending fellow,' though on reflection this reference to his business was not encouraging. He had a notion that a money-lender was usually a rich man.

Mr. Montgomery looked with dismay on the prospect before him. But Saxton must be saved at whatever cost. The first cost was the demand upon him for an address to the electors. Literary composition did not come easily to him, and the preparation of his address cost him an anguished day. But it was out at last, flaming in bright blue letters over every square foot of wall or hoarding unappropriated by Gideon's address, which had got the start of twelve hours.

What troubled Mr. Montgomery further was Gideon's inconsiderateness in the matter of addressing the electors. The dissolution was not even achieved, much less was the writ issued. It would be time enough then to go through the nuisance of shaking hands with every man or woman one met in the street, and to face the torture of addressing public meetings. But Gideon rushed into all this with a light heart, and unfortunate Mr. Montgomery had to plod wearily after him.

O'Brien had now taken up his quarters in the town, and was pushing matters forward both with tact and energy. Mr. Tandy was hard at work, though he preferred to remain in the background, leaving public appearances to O'Brien. Jack Bailey was also in high feather. He did not like Gideon personally, and felt little interest in the great political struggle agitating the country. But a fight was a fight. Here was one ready to hand, and Jack flung himself into the fray with infectious ardour.

The 'Saxton Beacon' came out as a daily sheet, in supplement of the weekly issue, just big enough in size to report meetings at which Gideon spoke and a column for Jack to prance in.

This he did with an acute delight that charmed Gideon, amused the town, and wrung the soul of Mr. Montgomery. That estimable gentleman found himself morning after morning subjected to the most scathing inquisition, not only painful in itself, but calculated to prove fatal to the prospects of his candidature. O'Brien put Jack up to a thing or two, and in due course there appeared articles in the 'Beacon' setting forth the number of Mr. Montgomery's attendances at the House, the direction in which his votes were given, and the number of times he had spoken.

What was even a more efficacious commentary was one Jack derived from a list of the honourable gentleman's local contributions. These were limited in amount, and strictly Conservative in the lines followed. What Mr. Montgomery's father had given to, to that he would subscribe, but he would go no further. The sum total did not make an imposing return, and a throb of indignation ran through Saxton when it discovered how little it had subsisted on during the long term of Mr. Montgomery's tenure of the seat.

Nothing was said in the 'Beacon' of Gideon's benefactions; but at the Blue Lion, along the beach, at the Dog and Duck, wherever the electors congregated, there were emissaries of the Liberal candidate setting forth the tale of Gideon's generosity. This was well enough in the past, but in prospect its brilliance was such as to hopelessly shrivel up Mr. Montgomery's puny gifts.

Mr. Dumfy had come down a day or two after Captain O'Brien, and had also taken up his residence permanently in the borough, or until such time as the election was decided. O'Brien took up his quarters at the Blue Lion, and, as it was felt that Gideon was sufficiently represented there, Mr. Dumfy was told off to the Dog and Duck. He didn't like the change, the company being lower, and the gin not so good. But he had no choice, and there was compensation to be found in other directions. At the Blue Lion he was sometimes overpowered by the impetuosity of Mr. Firminger, the austerity of Mr. Griggs, the large voice of Mr. Burnap, or the historical reminiscences of Mr. Goldfinch. At the Dog and Duck he was a Triton among minnows.

By common consent he took the chair at the end of the long deal table at which the 'Longshore men sat—always with their jerseys on, their sea boots well greased, ready at a moment's notice to meet the emergency that hourly overhung them. To this end they would not sit down on a bench alongside the table. Each man had his particular stool or chair, and sat at all angles and in some uncomfortable position, ready to jump up at a signal and hasten to the post of danger or of labour.

Unlike the cosy parlour at the Blue Lion, the tap-room at the Dog and Duck was cheered by long flashes of silence. In the Blue Lion, if there ever was a pause in the conversation (which was not often), Mr. Goldfinch was ready to fill it up with reminiscences of '32. At the Dog and Duck the conversation was conducted in a leisurely manner, as became men accustomed to contrast the vastness of the ocean with the narrowness of life. If a man had anything to say, he said it in a drawling voice, and would sometimes in the middle of a sentence stop to fill his pipe, secure from interruption. When he had made an end of speaking no one else was in a hurry to take up the tale, and they were really grateful to Mr. Dumfy if, in view of their exhausted physical condition after a hard day's work on the beach,

he would assume the principal duty of making
the conversation.

This Mr. Dumfy did with pleasure to himself and satisfaction to the company. His
feelings with respect to Gideon were more
acute than those of Jack Bailey, who simply
despised him, and was impatient at his plati-
tudes and his assumption. Mr. Dumfy, on the
contrary, hated him with a hate the more
bitter because he was compelled to hide it
under a fawning manner. Nevertheless, he
desired to see Gideon member for Saxton. If
he could thereafter hold his place it would be an
increased honour to himself. At any rate, there
were in the process of the election pickings to
be had which must be earned with at least
some semblance of fidelity and zeal.

Mr. Dumfy therefore served his master
at the Dog and Duck with great skill. He
painted on the fancy of the 'Longshore men
brilliant, if shadowy, pictures of advantages to
be derived by them when they should have

Gideon for a member instead of Mr. Montgomery.

At an early stage of his residence at the Dog and Duck, Mr. Dumfy had made clear one point that greatly exercised the minds of the 'Longshore men. They had heard something of Gideon's caution with respect to keeping clear of the Law, and began to tremble for their statutory 3*l.* Gideon, of course, had never heard of such a thing—certainly he had never discussed it. But Mr. Tandy had had a conversation with Captain O'Brien, which resulted in certain communications being made to the Conscript Fathers, who thereupon declared that the last vestige of doubt was removed, and that Gideon was as good as member.

Mr. Dumfy had apparently received a communication of the same kind, for on the second night he took the chair at the Dog and Duck every man in the room knew that his 3*l.* was safe.

Their minds being relieved from pressing anxiety, they were able to turn with undiminished vigour to the question of how they might also get 3*l.* from the other side.

Almost to a baccy box the 'Longshore men were with Gideon. They had not forgotten his genial bearing in the first weeks of his visits to the town, which they contrasted with the standoffishness or even more offensive condescension of Mr. Montgomery. Besides, Gideon was a benefactor. If it had not been for him there would have been no contest, and not a penny would have been spent in the town. There is a sturdy honesty in the breasts of all Englishmen, and this now asserted itself in favour of doing the right thing by Gideon.

At the same time if they could only get 3*l.* from the other side and add it to Gideon's retainer it would be a good and desirable thing.

Accordingly when Mr. Montgomery's agents began to stir and visited the beach, looked in at the Dog and Duck, and called upon these mariners of England at their own homes, they were so well received that grave doubt was cast on the assertion of Mr. Muffleton that the 'Longshore men had been bought by the enemy.

'They are good honest fellows after all,' Mr. Montgomery said, walking up and down his library with elastic step, and re-fixing his stock with a pleased air. 'I don't mind confessing that it would cut me to the heart to be left in the lurch by these simple, honest creatures, lured by a money-lending fellow. But they are faithful and honest, and mean to stand by the Constitution.'

CHAPTER XXII.

THE FLAGSTAFF AT THE BLUE LION.

THE dissolution took place on the 24th of March. Before the end of the week the writ had come down, and Roger Montgomery, Esq., gentleman, of the Hall, Saxton, and Gideon Fleyce, Esq., gentleman, of Carlton Street, London, were duly nominated as candidates. The proceedings at the nomination were of a melancholy character, the colour being deepened by Mr. Goldfinch, who shook his head all down High Street, and contrasted, for the information of any one who would stop to listen, the difference between ' this hole-and-corner business in a room ' and the glorious doings of '32, when the candidates stood out on the hustings in the light of day, and had dead cats, rotten eggs, and other evidences of political conviction thrown at them.

But though there were no cheerful proceedings at the hustings there was not lacking partial compensation. The wind was tempered to the shorn lamb by plentiful libations of beer and even of stronger drink.

The process by which this was obtained was exceedingly simple. Mr. Tandy, sitting quietly in his office and looking more respectable than ever, had on the day after the announcement of the dissolution despatched Mr. Burnap and Mr. Firminger to engage all the public-houses in the town in the interest of the Liberal candidate.

'That's what I call coming down on the block,' Mr. Firminger said as he went off gratefully on his mission.

This point of strategy was decidedly in advance of the Conservatives, who had yet scarcely wakened up to the energy of the opposition.

But that confidence in the honest Englishman which had cheered Mr. Montgomery when reviewing the action of 'Longshore men was now triumphantly vindicated. There were at least a dozen publicans who asked for twelve hours' consideration before accepting the retainer temptingly dangled before them by the commissioners of the Liberal candidate.

They urged various excuses for delay. They had a lodge meeting on or about that date ; their daughter was going to be married ; the house was about to be painted ; their wives ' were expecting ' about that time. Still they would see. Nothing would give them greater pleasure than to gratify so open-handed a gentleman as Mr. Fleyce. But they could not rightly say just now. The first thing in the morning, or perhaps before night-fall, they would send up word.

Both Mr. Burnap and Mr. Firminger knew well enough what this meant. These good men were not Liberals in politics, and though of course they would not allow political convictions to stand in the way of material gain, they would prefer, all other things being equal, to fly the blue flag over their doorway. As soon as the emissaries of the Liberal candidate were out of sight they with one accord rushed off to Mr. Muffleton to tell what was in the wind, and see if he meant to do the fair thing. If he did he should have the house and welcome. If he didn't they had said nothing that would drive custom from their door when tendered from the other side.

Mr. Muffleton was greatly upset by these horrid proceedings. Through forty years he had been accustomed to conduct the election proceedings for the Hall, and they had gone forward in a quiet, respectable manner. Now they were going with a rush that threatened to take Mr. Muffleton off his legs, and caused him heartily to wish that some one else would look after the business. But he was in for it and must go through with it, and the first thing was to engage these public-houses and any others that might be available.

Mr. Montgomery was very wroth when he heard what had been done, or rather what had been left undone.

'I am afraid we are muddling this dreadfully, Muffleton,' he said with a voice and a look that clearly intimated that though he said 'we' he meant 'you.' 'Here we are with only a dozen public-houses, and they have got, I suppose, between thirty and forty. What else are they up to?'

'Well,' said Mr. Muffleton, nervously polishing his gold-rimmed spectacles, 'I hear they are making open house all over the place. The landlords have instructions to serve any man with drink who calls and mentions Mr. Tandy's name. It's horrible, terrible, quite demoralising. I don't know what we must do.'

'I'll tell you what we must do,' said Mr. Montgomery fiercely, being, like most large-boned, phlegmatic men, very noisy in his wrath, 'we must do the same. It's no use beating about the bush or splitting hairs in Saxton. My father and my grandfather did this, and that hypocritical Tandy knows very well that it is the only way to carry an election in this borough when once blood is stirred up by an interloper like this money-lending fellow. He is spending money like water, and so shall I. See to that, Mr. Muffleton.'

'But there's the law,' said Muffleton, with growing uneasiness.

'The law be damned,' cried Mr. Montgomery, with a fine frankness, taking the oath as readily as if it had been proffered him in due form by the clerk at the table of the House of Commons. 'The law is all very well in its place, but its place is not Saxton at election times. What should we do if we stood by the law? This fellow would get in to a dead certainty. We should petition, and then there would come out such a story that would lead to the place being disfranchised, and we'd lose it out of the family. He's deep enough in the mire now, and dare not move against us. It will be a stand-up fight, and I mean to stand to it. Of course,' he added hastily, lowering his voice and changing his tone, 'these are only general instructions. You will understand, Mr. Muffleton, I don't want to go into any particulars or to know anything, except that you are devoting all your attention to the business. For my part, I am aware that contested elections are expensive things. You may depend upon it any money that may be necessary will 'be forthcoming. Only we must hold the seat.'

It was quite true what Mr. Muffleton had said about the instructions given to public-house keepers. The doors were thrown wide open, and Saxton had the biggest, longest drink within the memory of man. The 'Longshore men almost deserted the beach, and it is a merciful providence that nothing happened whilst they were away. Night and day the tap-room of the Dog and Duck was filled. Mr. Dumfy was not always in the chair, being engaged in various parts of the town, but he came in at night and presided in his usual place, and took his share of the good things going.

What troubled Saxton chiefly was the brief spell of the joyous interlude. It was only in the beginning of the month that the dissolution was announced. In the last week of the month it actually took place, and within a fortnight all would be over. This was the skeleton in the cupboard, which rattled its ghastly chain through every hour of the day and night, and bade the burgesses drink whilst the taps were running. All trade in the town was at a standstill—all save the great business of eating and drinking and shouting.

Some of the more provident among the free and independent electors, recognising the transitory nature of present joys, diligently sought opportunity for laying up stores of hard cash. The 3*l.* was safe and certain. It was, indeed, as good as in their pockets. But there should be other ways of adding to their store, and one was found in the erection of flagstaffs. Flags were illegal, but there was no law against flag-staffs, and presently these were erected before all the committee rooms, and, as Jack Bailey said, 'Saxton scudded under bare poles.'

This was the 'Longshore men's opportunity, and they made the most of it. It was a cheering spectacle to see them working outside the Blue Lion, where it was determined to erect the loftiest pole ever seen. Its proportions were magnificent, and so was the little account of the 'Longshore men.

'Twenty-five-pounds!' exclaimed Gideon, happening to see the item in Mr. Dumfy's account.

Dumfy's account was the only one he looked to, and that for reasons sufficient in themselves, though not gratifying to Mr. Dumfy. But Mr. Dumfy had not lived with the Spider for nothing. He had in this matter laid a trap for Gideon, and chuckled as he saw him falling into it. There were a good many items of his account which would not stand inquiry. As it happened this one would, Mr. Dumfy actually having paid over 25*l.* to Long Bill, the captain of the 'Longshore gang.

Now when Gideon fixed his eye shrewdly upon him, Mr. Dumfy displayed such marked uneasiness, that Gideon, throwing aside his caution, determined to look into the matter. It was not the 25*l.* that bothered him. He had a not unfounded suspicion that Dumfy was lining his own nest, and he thought if he detected him in this, it would have the effect of frightening him into honesty, since he would never feel sure that Gideon would not unexpectedly come in, put his finger on a particular item, and demand explanation.

'Who did you pay the money to?' he asked.

To Long Bill,' answered Mr. Dumfy, with a guilty air that sat well upon him.

'Go and tell him I want him. No—stop—'

and Gideon rang the bell. 'Send a messenger for Long Bill,' he said, when the waiter appeared. 'You can stay here, Mr. Dumfy, we will see this matter out.'

The messenger found Long Bill working very hard, with his hands deep set in his trousers pockets, his legs crossed and his body inclined at a comfortable angle, supported by the flagstaff, which he was convinced was the glory of Saxton, and would triumphantly propel Mr. Fleyce into Parliament. Bill had a short clay pipe in his mouth, and was plunged in profound meditation, besides suffering from the languor which steals over the body after an extraordinary physical effort. The flagstaff had now been up two days, but still Bill felt the effect of the unwonted exertion.

Summoned to meet the candidate, he thrust his pipe into his waistcoat pocket, unmindful of the circumstance that the sod was burning, and cheerfully followed the messenger. He felt sure it was something about the flagstaff, and hoped the interview would not begin and end in empty compliments. If there was a pound or two more going Bill felt he had earned it.

'Well, Bill, how are things going at the beach?' said Gideon, in his cheerful manner.

'Fust rate, sir,' said Bill, holding on to the top of the door as if it was a plank upon which · he had providentially come when battling with the waves. 'There's not a man of them as won't come up to the poll right and proper. The other party has been around talking of what's to be had. But them men's all as true as the sun when you are taking a hobservation. There's old Bowsprit says this very morning, "If they were to offer us 4*l.* a vote agen Mr. Fleyce's 3*l.* do you think we'd take it?" and every man of us said "No!"'

'Bowsprit?' said Gideon, reflectively; 'is he a voter? I don't know him by name.'

'It's Jack Files, your honour. We call him Bowsprit on account of his nose, which runs sheer out, and would be handy if he was to run agen a sea wall with wind and tide behind him. Of course you know,' Bill added, letting go the door the more fully to devote both hands to holding his hat by the brim and turning it round incessantly, as if it were, somehow, connected with his mental machinery, which had to be worked like a capstan, 'there's no knowing what's in men's minds, an' if so be as the other party *was* to offer 'em 4*l.* we might lose a vote or two. Praps your honour would think whether it was worth your while to go, say, to 3*l.* 10*s.* You'll be snug under the lee then, for there's not a man of 'em as 'ud let the ten shillings stand atween yer honour and the Houses of Parlyment.'

'I have not the slightest idea of what you are talking about,' said Gideon, smilingly, and looking the honest tar straight in the eyes. 'If it is anything about election expenses you must see Mr. Tandy. What I sent for you was about the flagstaff. I am thinking of having one put up at the Castle, and just wanted to know how much did you charge for this one.'

'Well, your honour, to speak right out, we got 25*l.* for it.'

Gideon was taken aback at this confirmation of Mr. Dumfy's honesty, and looked sharply at that injured individual to see if any signals had been passed to the gentleman before him who smelt so strongly of tar combined with a savour that Gideon thought was stale tobacco, but was really the pipe smouldering in his waistcoat pocket.

Mr. Dumfy, however, was ready for this, and had carefully placed himself full in Gideon's view, and with his back slightly turned to the ancient mariner.

Gideon had evidently made a false step, and there was nothing to be done but to follow up the inquiry on its natural lines.

'That's a great deal, isn't it?'

'Well, I don't know, yer honour. It don't come to much when you make it over amongst twenty-three hard-working men, all fathers of families, and every man of them got a vote.'

' But you don't mean to say it took twenty-three men to put up that pole?'

' 'Deed it did, yer honour, and took us three days into the bargain, three days of sweating and working that would have broke us down only for the drops of drink we got.'

' But what did the twenty-three men do?'

' Well, the fust thing we did was to get a flagstaff worthy of yer honour and Mr. Gladstone. So we goes all over the town looking one up. That took us a good couple of hours, and we dropped into a house or two on the way, and said a word for yer honour to any gentleman who was taking a drop. We found a flagstaff at Mr. Burnap's, but it looked quite poor like; not worth having. We was awful tired by this time, but I says to the chaps :— " This has got to be done, so we'll have another gallon of beer, and down this comes." We was feeling a little queer with the walking

round and the sun, and didn't do any more the
fust day than dismantle the fust flagstaff as we
put up. At night, down at the Dog and Duck,
where the gemman here stops, we had a talk
over the thing, and I says to the chaps :—
" We're going to fix the biggest flagstaff here
as was ever seen in the town, one that the
mounseers over the way might see if the day
was bright, and they kep their weather eye
open. We're going to beat them Tories on this
tack." So we goes and gets a ship mast, sixty
or seventy feet high, and a pretty good weight
as yer honour may guess. The next thing
we got was a scaffold pole that reached from
the ground right up to the other side of the
houses—it might be forty-five feet, that was to
go on the top of it ; then we had to get the
gallant mast. Then we had to get two iron
caps, and they was of the weight of about three
hundredweight. It is eighty feet high. It
has to go above all the rest, and above all the
houses, and they could see it over the way at

Bullong. Now the great question was, we had come to Mr. Burnap's to get a pair of shears to rig it. When we went down to Mr. Burnap he had got no shears. What does we have to do? We had to dismantle our luggers to get these shears, and unrig all our masts and get our flags and ropes to get this up. Now, it is no little weight to get it up, because it is eighty or ninety feet when it is up. We dismantled our two boats, that is our big luggers, and a tidy job it was for a score of men, and a dry un too.'

'And it took twenty-three men all this time?' asked Gideon.

'Yes, yer honour, and working pretty well. Moreover than which look where we'd ha' been when we'd dismantled our masts; suppose anything had come on the bank and we with our luggers dismantled. Where 'ud we ha' been, sir?'

'Well, probably you would have been at the Dog and Duck,' said Gideon, smiling genially. 'But you will understand I am not quarrelling with you or disputing your work or wages. I only wanted to know about having a pole put up at the Castle on the day after the election.'

'We'll do it, sir, and we'll do it right and proper, only o' course yer honour 'll find us a pole, 'cause it 'll never do for our luggers to be dismantled, and the wind likely to blow on shore at any moment.'

'All right, Bill, we will bear that in mind. Good morning.'

'Good morning, yer honour,' said Bill, sending his hat round with increased velocity, and examining the rim with added intensity, but making no sign of other motion.

'I will let you know about the pole,' Gideon repeated.

'Thank 'er, sir, but I was just thinking yer honour would like me to drink yer health.'

'I should indeed, Bill, but I want you fellows to understand that I could not give you a drop of beer if you were parched. The law won't have it, Bill, and the law must be obeyed.'

'Perhaps Mr. Bill would do a walk with me,' said Mr. Dumfy. 'I'm going towards the Dog and Duck.'

The cloud that had gathered over the bronzed and furrowed brow of Long Bill cleared off at this invitation. He was a slow-witted man, not trained in fine distinctions. He had often heard of this determination on the part of Gideon not to stand treat for any man. It seemed from the abundance of liquor all over the place that he had at one time gone back from this resolution. But it was Mr. Tandy's name that was used as the open sesame, at which the hospitable doors flew back. Long Bill knew enough of Mr. Tandy to feel convinced that his benevolence did not take this promiscuous shape. It must have been Mr. Fleyce, and now, as he reported at the Dog and Duck, with some slight verbal inaccuracy, he 'had heern him with his own voice say as he couldn't stand him twopenn'orth of anythin' hot.'

A gleam of intelligence shot across his mind as Mr. Dumfy interposed. There was something going on that he could not quite understand. But the liquor was not to be stopped, and so long as Bill got that he was not inclined to disturb himself with speculation as to whose hand turned the tap.

CHAPTER XXIII.

MEDITATION AMONG THE PEWS.

IT was not only the 'Longshore men who were taken aback by the swiftness with which the days passed and brought on the crisis at Saxton. Gideon felt it with what he was beginning to regard as overwhelming force. Everything was going on swimmingly in his outward relations with the electors. There was no question of his popularity over that of the old member. His meetings were more crowded and enthusiastic. He was exceedingly pleased with his own fluent speech, and it seemed that the kind of oratory was not less agreeable to his hearers.

Mr. Montgomery floundered through his commonplaces and stale denunciation of the Opposition, and repeated many familiar phrases in exaltation of the foreign policy of Lord Beaconsfield. Gideon fought shy of the question of foreign policy, partly because he knew nothing about it, but largely because he was shrewd enough to see that it was not of the smallest possible interest to the people of Saxton The great question for them was the 3*l.* to be paid for their votes. That being assured, they felt that the safety and honour of England rested upon a rock, into whatsoever hands the chances of the forthcoming election might place the destinies of the country.

Gideon had a difficulty, one by no means unfamiliar in daily life. He had spent a great deal of money during the last year in miscellaneous ways, and there had been a pull upon him for Mr. Burnap's bill, and for the account of Mr. Griggs. These had been no small items, and in addition there had been the weekly expenses of his household. He had practically given up business in Carlton Street, which was accordingly closed as a source of revenue. All his own fortune and that of some others were invested in his land schemes. These still continued to look prosperous, and promised at no distant time to realise for him a vast fortune as the result of his foresight and shrewdness.

In the meantime there were large sums to be paid quarterly in the way of interest, and there was no way of obtaining these except by fresh borrowing.

That was a circle which by this time had become a pathway sore to the foot and searing to the soul. One after another he had closed the sources of accommodation, of course in each case adding to the weight of his quarterly responsibilities. He was paying immense sums in interest, and it so happened that quarter day was again at hand. He had a good sum in the bank, but within a hundred or two every penny of it was pledged in payment of interest. Under ordinary circumstances this would not have mattered.

What particularly pressed upon him now

was this 3*l.* a-piece wanted on behalf of the free and independent electors. There was a good deal of money flowing day by day, accounts opened with public-houses, with the printer, and with the agents. Till the election was over these might stand. But 3,000*l.* was wanted within the next week to pay down on the nail the 3*l.* each which the electors regarded as their due, and without which they certainly would not go to the poll, or, what was worse, would go and vote for his opponent.

He must have the 3,000*l.* within a week. This he said to himself, and with his old Napoleonic manner; but when he came to think where he was to get it from his views became a little less decided.

In addition to the money wanted by the voters, Gideon had coming on within a few days a great fête at Castle Fleyce, to which he had invited the nobility and gentry of the county, or rather such of them as professed Liberal politics. He yearned to see himself at the head of a table in a real though restored castle, entertaining the Lord-Lieutenant of the county and many of the county gentry. He had suggested this to O'Brien, though studiously keeping in the background all other motives except that of political expediency.

'We must show that we have the party with us,' he said, and O'Brien had agreed, though a little dubiously.

The Captain broached the subject to Sir Henry Gilbert, who had his hands full enough, amongst other occupations the prospect of a contest in his own borough being forced upon him. But Sir Henry had, as he had promised, looked into affairs at Saxton, and saw a rare chance of winning an old Tory seat. He would spare no effort to secure it, and accordingly wrote a letter to the Lord-Lieutenant, who happened to be a Liberal, commending Gideon to his judicious care, and urging him to accept his proposed invitation.

This the Lord-Lieutenant had done with

gracious warmth, and Gideon, after having given the fact time and opportunity to permeate through the county circles, had issued invitations to every one, who was anybody at all and a Liberal, to a luncheon party at the Castle.

The invitation had been accepted with flattering unanimity, and Gideon had before him the prospect of a pleasing day. But this also would cost money, and it must be ready money, since it plainly would not do for a candidate for Parliamentary honours, whose chief recommendation was his great wealth, to begin opening accounts with tradespeople.

The money must be had, and Gideon would have it; but where from? He parted with bits of his improving land with an anguish that marked the taint of the Spider's blood, and which, if it had been known in Fulham Road, where a good deal else was known, might have done something to close the breach between himself and his father.

Every rood of land he sold now he knew he was parting with at a sacrifice. If he could only hold on a couple of years, or a year more, the land would be worth fifty per cent. more than to-day. Whatever he sold now by so much he lost the fruits of his speculation.

It was no use going to the great banks which had already advanced him large sums on the title-deeds of his estate. It was just possible they might make what was comparatively a small advance. But the application for it would create suspicion that would have inevitable consequences. Very possibly no one of the banks knew to what extent Gideon was obliged to the other.

So long as he wore his heart upon his sleeve and a smile upon his lips, and looked so rosy and prosperous and careless, and especially while he didn't attempt to narrow the margin which the bankers had left on the value of the property in order to cover themselves, all would be well and the time would pass pleasantly till the arrival of the happy hour when he could begin to re-sell his land and reduce the capital account.

He turned this thing over in his mind as he sat in his pew at the old church on the hill, whilst the curate ran through the exordium of the morning service. It was a rare old church in spite of the fearful process of renovation it had undergone. Nothing could take away from its appearance when viewed from the outside. Within, the old pews had long ago disappeared, and open benches of light oak had taken their places.

In one of these Gideon sat. He had found out which pew had pertained to the Castle in olden times, and, finding it in the possession of a prosperous retired grocer, he bought it for a large sum. He had it all to himself, though he had furnished it in a generous manner suitable for contingencies. The cushions ran the full length of the bench, and so did the Turkey carpet on the floor, whilst handsomely bound

Bibles, prayer-books, and hymn-books were strewn about the shelves.

Just facing Gideon was a tablet, sacred to the memory of Richard Montgomery, member of the Long Parliament. Gideon had not at first liked close proximity to this testimony of unquestionable antiquity established for his opponent, contrasting painfully with his own newness. In time, as things prospered with his canvass, he grew to be pleased with this reminder of the greatness of the victory he was about to achieve.

Not only would he win for the Liberal party a borough which had long been an appendage of the enemy, but the man whom he was about to dispossess was a member of a family rooted in the county for centuries. That he, single-handed, should achieve such a triumph, seemed to him a strong recommendation for high favour with his party. They could not take him into the Ministry yet, he admitted; but that would come by-and-bye, and it would find him wealthy, with a unique country seat, and the means of providing himself with a town house.

On the other side of the aisle in the front seat were half a dozen old men of wonderful ages. They lived in the almshouses, in considerable terror of Knut, seeing that no one about to leave his house could be sure that this was not the very moment at which the dog might be taking his constitutional, and might knock him over, even as he had floored Mr. Dumfy. They had contracted a habit of cautiously surveying the street before emerging, and this they did the more particularly on Sunday, when they were dressed in their best, in neat brown coats with fine brass buttons, and a blue stock, which, if need were, dispensed with the necessity of a collar.

One or two of them had ear-trumpets, which they lifted with strange persistency towards the pulpit to catch the thin stream of commonplace which the curates in turn ejected at a tremendous pressure, as if the congregation before them were aflame with sin, and they were putting the fire out.

Gideon often looked at these old gentlemen, and wondered what their past history might have been. They were all tall men, and had been stalwart. Even now their cheeks were rosy as a winter apple, and it was evident they had not been driven to this place by stress of ill-health.

Looking over at them, his eye fell upon a pew, a little in the rear, in which sat three familiar figures. There was Mr. Tandy at the head, comfortably dressed in black, with gold-rimmed spectacles on his nose, and a large prayer-book firmly held in both hands.

Gideon felt it was worth something to have a man of that kind in his service. He seemed to diffuse an atmosphere of respectability for a considerable radius. It was so far-reaching that it caught even Jack Bailey, the third figure

from the end of the pew, counting from that at
which Mr. Tandy sat.

Gideon could not make out what Jack
should be doing there. He knew very well
why he (Gideon) should go to church. It was
the proper thing to do, and was expected of
him, not only as a candidate for the representation of the borough, but as the owner of the
Castle. Jack had no such calls upon him, and,
indeed, it was only within the last week or two
he had developed a tendency towards taking part
in the service.

He had, with quite a touching diffidence,
one day asked Mr. Tandy for permission to
sit in his pew occasionally, a permission
readily granted since there was plenty of room,
and Jack was a favourite with Mr. Tandy, who
was glad to see him taking this turn, having the
impression that when he lived in London he was
a little wild.

Jack was a credit to his early bringing up,
as he stood—not quite so near the end of

the pew as he might have done—with a book in his hand, singing a great deal better than Mr. Tandy did.

It was Napper who held the middle place, and whose presence seemed to draw Jack towards the upper end of the pew in a manner which he, becoming suddenly conscious of, from time to time, overcame by taking a long stride that landed him at the remote end. He took several strides during the course of a moderately short service, though he was unconscious of any physical action by which he edged up towards Miss Tandy till he trembled with sweet delight at finding that his elbow touched hers with ever so slight an impact.

Napper did not seem to notice this recurring accident, perhaps because she had got used to it, as one in time gets used to the regular ticking of a clock. But Jack never failed to blush violently, and, under pretence of arranging a book or of turning to look back, he got clear away to the other end.

Gideon noticed his presence with a general idea that he was not after any good. There was some girl about, probably Miss Nethersoll. Or perhaps he was a little weary of his usual companions at the Blue Lion, and had looked in to steep himself in the respectability of the parish church. Of his real motive Gideon had not the slightest suspicion. He had now in his own mind come to regard it as a matter of course that Napper would become his wife. He had not seen so much of her of late, he believed because he had been exceptionally busy; but he was also conscious of some determined drawing off on her part. When he had suggested a visit to the Castle she had been busy, and when in his old manner he had asked for advice upon some particular point, she had protested that the matter was one of which she knew nothing.

But this, if he thought of it at all, he put down to maidenly reserve, the exhibition of which all the more recommended her to him.

Of course she could not expect to look so high. She had been misled by his earlier manner, when, not being in any way serious, he had been excessively devoted. When she found him drawing off, she, like the fine, good-natured girl she was, drew back also.

Gideon liked her the better for this, and now, insensibly soothed by the quietness of the place, broken only by the thin, artificially pitched voice of the curate, or by the solemn notes of the organ, his thoughts took on a further tenderness towards the girl. He felt that he was really getting very fond of her, and for the moment grew impatient for the coming of the time when King Cophetua might take the beggar maid by the hand. She was, he thought, growing even more beautiful than ever.

She was certainly less lively, and had taken to look at things through sad eyes which greatly puzzled him.

CHAPTER XXIV.

CLOUDING OVER.

THE fact is Napper was sick at heart with shame and humiliation at the things going on in Saxton. It had all come upon her as a surprise, a circumstance which attested her youth and innocence. Mr. Goldfinch could have enlightened her, but she didn't care for Mr. Goldfinch, holding him to be a tiresome person who sold indifferent tea, and devoted to gossip hours that would have been better employed in selecting superior samples of sugar.

Napper had evolved from her own fancy a brilliant picture of Saxton asserting its own right, and, when coarse and dirty hands thrust themselves forward and daubed the canvas, she was first indignant, then dazed, and finally sorry, with that worst of sorrows in which is mingled a feeling of shame.

It was the fault originally of her nature, and next of her self-education, that she was accustomed to accept words and phrases with their simple and literal meanings. Confined within the narrow limits of a country town, with little society beyond that of her father, whom she completely dominated, Napper's sympathy had gone out with eager, widespread arms to welcome the good and true. She had known that politics formed a science the object of which was the amelioration of the lot of mankind. What did people do in Parliament if they did not do good?

Conservatives and Liberals to Napper's untutored mind were simply distinctive names for two parties equally anxious to do good to their fellow-men. It was much the same as if one had been christened Edmund and the other Henry.

The House of Commons was an assemblage

of men of conspicuous ability, either born to great wealth or, having achieved it, patriotically devoting their leisure to the good of the commonwealth. It is an odd indication of Napper's fancy that she pictured to herself the House of Commons filled by elderly gentlemen of benevolent aspect, with white beards, and many of them bald.

When Gideon was introduced to her as a candidate for parliamentary honours, she was conscious of a slight shock at his comparative youthfulness. But, as she argued with herself, that was a thing that would mend. Of course, being a young member, Gideon, if elected, would not take any prominent part in the business of the House. He would sit and hear his elders respectfully, seizing every opportunity of taking counsel with them.

The House of Commons, as being the focus of all that was actively good in the nation, had always possessed over Napper a strong attraction. Thus, when she found herself in the company of Mr. Montgomery, she availed herself of the opportunity of talking about the place, and so acquired bits of personal information that would seem abstruse to ladies outside the parliamentary circle. She knew about the terrace on which members walked, and pictured to herself Gideon strolling up and down there drinking in counsel from his elders.

She had read that Aristotle conveyed his valuable lessons whilst walking up and down, and perhaps the terrace had been specially designed in imitation of the promenade in the Lyceum at Athens.

Then there was the tea-room, a cosy place, as she imagined it, where members, refreshed and invigorated with Bohea, talked matters over, and discussed their next move for the public good. Her fancy had, in short, built itself a lordly dwelling-house, where members of Parliament lived in company with all the Virtues.

So deeply rooted was this feeling of reverence for all connected with the Legislature that it was some time before Gideon succeeded in breaking through the armour of respect with which she had environed him. He did it at last. But at worst, Napper thought here was one who had mistaken his vocation.

It was highly creditable that he should think he could be a member of Parliament, and could join the unselfish, single-minded, patriotic assembly at Westminster. We often make mistakes when considering our own possibilities. Gideon had made a grievous one, though perhaps if he succeeded in getting into Parliament he would in due course be influenced by the atmosphere he was privileged to breathe, and would by the time he did so grow white-bearded and bald-headed, and be as unselfish, as honest, and as intelligent as the rest.

Then came the contest, which Napper watched with feelings settling down from bewilderment into shamed despair. It pained her most to know that her father was reputed to be the principal agent in working out the infamy that had fallen on the town. Where all was so bad, so hopeless for the country, and so disgraceful to her native town, Napper felt that she would be selfish if she dwelt too much on a matter personal to herself. She ceased to mention the subject to her father, who saw with pain the estrangement growing up between himself and the girl who was more a companion than a child to him.

Mr. Tandy was overwhelmed with work, and had never ten minutes to spare; but he would have gladly given half an hour to Napper if she had proposed to go back to the old dancing lessons, or to the essays in singing which, painful even to Knut, she had always submitted to with infectious merriment.

But Napper had neither heart to dance nor voice to sing now. Of course she didn't sulk, and a stranger unaccustomed to the ordinary relations of father and daughter would have thought nothing was lacking in her attention or affectionate respect.

But Mr. Tandy knew it, and felt it very deeply.

When the public-houses were first thrown open and Napper walking about the town met some of her old friends amongst the 'Longshore men, and other more industrious members of the community, unduly elated and evidently idling the time which they should have spent for the support of their families, she stopped and .talked to them with grave voice and reproachful look. But they explained that it was election time. The other side must not get in on any account, and for their parts they were prepared at whatever sacrifice to do their duty.

Napper, recognising the hopelessness of the case, presently ceased to take any active part in the struggle, and went through the town as little as possible. In the afternoon she and Knut went out for long strolls through lanes where the hedgerows were beginning to open their eyes to the fact that spring was at hand. Also she went down to the beach, where Knut resumed with unimpaired energy his personal difference with the sea, which, even when the tide was ebbing, sent in an occasional wave that wet his forepaws and resulted in a torrent of indignant remonstrance and command.

Jack Bailey would gladly have sacrificed the interests of the ' Beacon ' to the opportunity of accompanying Napper on these excursions. He had, in fact, made advances in that direction which surprised him by their modesty. But Napper had put him aside in an unmistakable manner.

If she had reminded him that the interests of an important journal rested upon his shoulders, and that they were neglected by absence from the office at particular hours, Jack might have found means to overcome such arguments. What was the ' Beacon ' or a whole coastline of beacons compared with the delight of talking for an hour with Napper, whilst he found occupation for Knut in throwing about sticks which the dog tore to the last shred?

Napper liked Mr. Bailey's company well enough in its way, and was encouraged thereto by the strong preference shown for him by Knut. Knut plainly disliked Mr. Dumfy, though not going the length of actively and forcibly hating him. Gideon he simply endured, it being no particular business of his if his mistress found pleasure in his company. But for Jack he had suddenly conceived that honest liking, the possibility of which was similarly demonstrated on his early acquaintance with Napper herself. Next to Napper he plainly loved Jack better than any of his acquaintances among mankind.

This was a strong recommendation to Napper on Jack's behalf, but it was not strong enough to induce her to be bothered with Jack's company when she wanted her own.

'Thank you, Mr. Bailey,' she had said when Jack had proposed to accompany her, 'I would rather go alone.'

There was no getting over that. It was exactly what Napper meant, and Jack knew it when she spoke the words. So he went down to the office, took off his coat, had in a pint of stout, lit his pipe, and, inspired by those ambrosial delights, proceeded to 'scarrify Montgomery.'

All this was dark to Gideon, who was able on quite other grounds to explain why Napper was silent and *distraite*. It was because she was not sure of his intentions. Gideon was convinced of this, and felt pleased with the thought of how delighted she would be when the veil was removed.

That would be when more important calls of business were disposed of, when he was member for Saxton, and his big transactions were running smoothly and safely.

But what if disaster were to overtake him

at the critical moment; if, just as his hand were reached out to take the prize, his arm should shrivel up?

Long unaccustomed to difficulties in money matters, and confident in his own resources, he had let this temporary pressure fall lightly upon him. It would be met somehow as other difficulties had been met. But sitting here in his newly furnished pew, and looking over at Napper, there suddenly came upon him a fearful thought of the possibility of evil.

It was quite certain he would not win his election unless 3,000*l.* in hard cash were forthcoming within the next ten days. This was not a question in which credit could be considered. He saw, as if an abyss had suddenly opened before him, how all his credit depended upon this one thing. His fortunes were being built up on the principle of a row of bricks set edgewise without mortar. Being scientifically placed, so long as no one gave a kick at either end they would stand. But should he fail at Saxton he felt it would be a blow that would utterly upset him and leave him unable to cope with difficulties elsewhere that required a cool hand and supple wrist.

Where should he turn for the help that must be forthcoming immediately? He had withdrawn his eye from the pew in which Napper sat, and leaning back in his seat was wrestling with this thought. He did not notice that the congregation had risen, and it was only the sound of the organ that startled him from his reverie.

In choirs and places where they sing here followed the anthem, and Gideon, with something of a scared mind, listened to the well-trained choir as they sang 'I will arise and go to my Father.'

It was a strange coincidence, and Gideon, though by no means of a superstitious nature, thought there was something in it. After his last visit to Fulham Road, he had, in his businesslike way, put outside his calculations the possibility of any help from his father. He knew the old man, and he knew that when he said if he were starving he would not give him a penny he meant what he said. But, after all, that might be a mere ebullition of passion. He could not be insensible to the advantage accruing to the family if his son succeeded in forcing his way to an upper place among the gentry.

Besides, as Gideon felt, he had two strings to his bow. He should appeal to his father on the ground of affection and family ties. That, he felt, was a cord of somewhat feeble fibre. The other one, more to be relied upon, was the undeniable security he could offer for a temporary loan. And it would be well worth his while to pay whatever interest his father might demand.

What followed of service or sermon Gideon had not the slightest idea. He was turning over in his mind the prospects of the step he had now decided to take. The more he thought of it the better he liked it. His father had abundance of spare cash which he would like to put out to usury. Gideon had seen it in his safe, a vision of which, with its little packets of sovereigns, rose before his mind, obscuring the pulpit, the pew in which Napper sat, the tablet in the wall recording the births and deaths and achievements of his early predecessor in the representation of Saxton—shutting out everything.

Why should his father have wealth like that, so easily accessible, when his son was in difficulties, even in danger of losing everything? Gideon's eyes glistened with a new light as he stared straight into the visionary safe. It was almost as much his as his father's, and was at the present time no good to anybody.

There was no time to be lost, and Gideon would go off to town by the first train. He could get out to Fulham, and be back by the last train, which slipped a carriage at the junction.

He need not say anything to any one of his journey. It was purely business of his own, essentially a family transaction. Why should any one know even that he had gone up to London? But Gideon was a little irritable after his profound contemplation, indulged in whilst one of the curates read out the Litany, and the other twittered a few commonplaces from the pulpit. He had not got over the chill that came upon him when he saw, as in a vision, the certain victory at Saxton snatched from him for the temporary lack of a few thousand pounds, and he was vexed with himself for the terror that had come upon him when he thought of the slight thread upon which his fortunes hung.

If he had told the servants at the Castle that he was going up to town, and would not be back till the last train, it would have been accepted as a matter of course, even cheerfully, as opening up unexpected prospect of unrestricted holiday. But Gideon snarled to himself with quite unwonted humour that they would be wondering what he was going for, perhaps guessing that he was going to beg a loan from his father—a personage of whose very existence they were in happy ignorance.

He thought he would make a hearty lunch, forego dinner, and have placed in his study some things that would do for supper when he came home at night.

He tried his best at the well-supplied luncheon table, but the things went away untasted.

' 'Ope you ain't ill, sir,' said Parker, the butler, who had been recommended to Gideon on high authority, and who had assumed somewhat magisterial airs in the new house.

' No, I ain't ill,' answered Gideon, turning upon the faithful retainer a look of unexpected and inexplicable ferocity that long lingered in his honest mind; ' and if I was ill and wanted you to know I would tell you. Now have these things cleared away. I shall not take any dinner to-night. I've got some writing to do, and don't want to be disturbed. Take into the study that chicken, some bread, and a bottle of claret. When I want anything I'll help myself, and if any one calls say I am not at home. Keep all noise and interruption away from the study. You can lock up at the usual time, and let the servants go to bed.'

Gideon sat by the study fire for an hour, buried in deep thought, which grew increasingly troubled. The very fact that he had but yesterday made light of his troubles now gave them quite exaggerated proportions. If his head had been as cool as usual he might have seen half a dozen ways of getting out of his difficulty preferable to that upon which he was now determined. But the excitement of the last week had begun to tell upon his health. He was, without knowing it, a little feverish. He had eaten little all day, and he rarely drank.

Parker noticed with surprise that he should have asked for a bottle of claret, knowing that his habitude was oftener to take water than indulge in even a single glass of wine. But Gideon had thought that he might come in tired, and a good glass of claret would refresh him.

There was an up-train which passed the Junction at five o'clock. He would catch that, be in town at half past six, see his father, get his business done, and be safely home again before midnight without any of the prying gossips of Saxton knowing that he had been out of his study. He would walk to the Junction gladly, feeling the need to work off in some way the excitement that possessed him.

His study was on the ground-floor, and facing it was the shrubbery with a pathway leading down to a gate by which he could reach the highway. The only point at which any servants who might be about could see him would be as he crossed the few feet of lawn before the study window, and walked across the carriage road, flanked on the other side by the shrubbery.

It would take him an hour to walk to the Junction, though he felt that in his present mood he would do it in much less time. It was a fine afternoon, though grey and chill. He would not even bother himself with an overcoat. Taking up a thick, knobbed stick, which was his constant companion in such walks as he found time to indulge in, he softly opened the study window and stepped out on to the grass.

There was no one about, the servants being on the other side of the Castle, engaged at the moment in discussing their master, and arguing a theory, put forward by Parker, that he might be taking to secret drinking and was about to begin mildly with a bottle of claret.

Gideon dropped the window softly, making sure that he could open it again, and, sauntering across the road into the shrubbery, entered the footpath.

Once clear from observation, he set off at a swinging pace in the direction of the railway station.

CHAPTER XXV.

THE PRODIGAL SON.

THE bells were ringing for evening service as Gideon's hansom drove along the Fulham Road in the direction of the bijou residence suitable for a bachelor of fortune. It was close upon the last stroke, and the well-dressed throng were hurrying forward with a pleasant bustle. It occurred to Gideon as he watched them whether after all their business was not preferable to his own. Why should he be thus harassed and placed in the position of a beggar at his father's door?

This last consideration was one that did not greatly afflict his soul—affecting him rather by the consideration that after all he might get nothing out of his father.

And what was it all for?. He was happy enough as long as he had been content to follow his father's business. He was brim full of joy in the excitement of carrying out his Napoleonic land policy. If he had only kept to the money-making all would have been well. It was this drain of carrying on the campaign in Saxton that was at the bottom of his present troubles. But for that he could easily have tided over the temporary period of difficulty, which arose whenever it was necessary to find the interest on the mortgages. He had spent a good deal of money and time at Saxton, and what was it for?

He meant to have his money's worth out of the House, not in the shape of gold, but in the way of social advancement and gratification. But when the prize was won would he after all enjoy it? He didn't care for dinner parties in any of their aspects. He didn't drink wine. Simple food agreed with him best, and as for conversation as he had sampled it at O'Brien's dinner they might as well have talked Greek.

Up to the present time what was certain was that he was spending a lot of money in keeping Saxton in drink, a thing which he abhorred, and providing means for that young jackanapes Bailey to swagger round the town and set himself up as a great authority. The paper was bleeding him to the tune of 10*l.* to 15*l.* a week, and so far as he could see all the advantage went to Jack.

He would stop this when the election was over, and Mr. Jack must bundle back to his garret in London and his habitual uncertainty about dinner.

All was black, or at best densely grey, whichever way he viewed it. If he could have arranged with the cabman, by giving him an extra sovereign, to drive him clear out of the radius of Saxton and the whole business, he would on the spur of the moment have produced the coin. But he was in for it now, and, shaking himself together, he determined to go through with it.

He would get this money from his father; within ten days he would be member for Saxton; and then he would begin to reap after all this painful sowing.

He dismissed the cab at the corner of the quiet and eminently respectable street which the bijou residence fronted, having at its rear, within a few feet, the backs of other houses. When Gideon was last at the house he had given a thundering ran-tan at the knocker. Now he tapped modestly, waiting patiently for any sign of response. He heard presently the shuffling of slippered feet along the hall. The door opened as far as the chain would permit, and there, framed in the aperture as formerly, he beheld the engaging countenance of his parent.

' Ain't you early? ' said the old gentleman, holding up the exceedingly thin tallow candle which wobbled in the not too capacious tin candlestick.

'It is me, father,' said Gideon, with a cheerful effort at a smile.

The look of slight annoyance on the old gentleman's face with which he responded to what he supposed was the too early call of an expected guest deepened into blazing anger.

'Oh, it's you, is it; what do you want?'

'Well, first I want to come in.'

'Then want will be your master,' said the old gentleman, and proceeded to close the door. But Gideon had his foot inside.

'Come, come, father,' he said, 'don't be so inhospitable. You would not turn your only son away when he comes to see you on a Sunday night.'

'He only comes to see me because he wants something,' retorted the old man suspiciously.

'Yes, father, I do want something. I want your advice, which I know I have neglected too long.'

'Ah, that's your little game, is it! Come

to me for advice, eh? I know what that means. A father's advice is usually written out on a cheque. But come in. I think I'd like to see how you look when you go away without the cheque. Come along; here's this candle guttering away in a wasteful manner. I suppose you've wax, and perhaps three or four burning at the same time. One does for your father, but then he hasn't to go about among his relations on a Sunday night begging.'

Thus pleasantly the old gentleman chirped as he led the way to the room that served him for everything but a bedchamber. It was just the same as Gideon had seen it before, except that now it looked somewhat more gloomy by the light of the solitary dip. There was a diminutive fire in the grate, made up on a principle long studied by the Spider, and brought to a high state of perfection. The grate being filled with slack, he let it burn only in the centre, directing with the poker little bits on the red heat as occasion required. This saved the slack, and found him occupation during the long evening.

There was a scuttle nearly full of the fuel by the side of the fireplace. On the grate Gideon saw a pan standing, and even fancied, though of course this was but fresh evidence of his fevered state of mind, that there was a savoury smell in the apartment as of meat being cooked. This impression seemed to be supported by the circumstance that a cloth (originally intended for a towel, but now adapted as a tablecloth suitable for a bachelor of fortune) was spread upon the table.

On a chair by its side were some plates and a knife and fork. The Spider had evidently been interrupted whilst in the act of laying the festive board.

'Didn't know you dined so late, father,' said Gideon, determined to be agreeable.

'No, I suppose you didn't. There's not much you do know of your father—what he does or how he lives. What are you staring at? The safe? Yes, there it is, and you know what's in it. I'll show you it again. It's a pretty sight for you aristocrats, and I dare say makes your mouth water.'

The old gentleman took the key out of his breast pocket, and after fumbling some time with the lock, as if he were not quite sure which way it turned, he pulled back the heavy doors, and, holding the tallow candle over his head, showed Gideon once more the neatly fastened rouleaux.

'There you are, sir. What d'ye think of that? Isn't that better than your lords and ladies, and castles, and Houses of Commons, and grand carriages, and prancing horses? They all cost money; these cost nothing to keep. Now what have you come for? Not to murder your old father, I do hope, and rob him of the earnings of an honest life. What are you doing with that stick? Put it down in the corner.'

'Don't be foolish, father,' said Gideon,

really angry at this untimely jest, which the old man enjoyed the more intensely as he saw how it annoyed his son.

'Oh, I'm not afraid of you, my boy, though a lad who is ashamed of his father's name and calling would not much mind putting him out of the way. See, I lock the safe, but I leave the key in it. You've not put the stick down yet,' and the old gentleman made a fresh feint of being in mortal terror.

'You always will have your joke, father,' said Gideon, putting the stick down in the corner of the room. 'I don't think they are always in the best taste, but you must be pretty lonely here, and the way you keep up your spirits is wonderful.'

'Yes, I'm pretty merry when I'm by myself, and, as I was thinking of having a cheerful evening, perhaps you will go as soon as you can. Now how much do you want? How much and when? I knew you would come to me in the end.'

Gideon had intended to lead up to the matter gently, and to prove, as was not difficult, that the needed loan was only temporary, and that there were no scruples in the matter of interest. But the old gentleman was so surprisingly businesslike there was no necessity for this circumlocution.

He had evidently made up his mind to let Gideon have the money, and the best move was to pacify him by acknowledging his remarkable prescience.

'You are a wonderful man, father,' he said, clearing away the crockery and seating himself at the table. 'There's no coming over you, or beating you in taking a long look ahead. The fact is, I did come round to talk with you about money matters.'

'Ah, ha,' cried the old gentleman, picking up a piece of tallow that had dropped into the candlestick, and placing it near the wick, so that it might add to the thin stream of nutriment. 'I thought it was only a friendly call, a sort of looking up your relations on a Sunday night, when you had nothing else to do ?'

'I would have been glad to do that, father, often enough, only you remember the last time I was here you forbade me the house, turned me out in fact.'

'Precisely, and you wouldn't come now if you didn't want to get something out of the old gentleman. Go on, squeeze me. What am I good for but that? Here's your lemon, squeeze it,' and the facetious old gentleman, cocking his velvet cap a little on one side, threw himself back in the chair and opened his arms wide in supposed representation of a lemon.

It was a very dry one, and certainly did not look as if it would repay the labour expended upon it. But to Gideon the affair was exceptionally hopeful.

'I am not going to squeeze you, or to ask you for anything I am not quite willing to pay handsomely for. The fact is, with all your

securities in the bank and your gold in the safe
I'm quite as rich as you.'

'Only you haven't got any money to carry
on your little game at Saxton. You have just
paid your interest on the mortgages, and now
you want your father to come down handsomely and help you to corrupt the electors of
this precious borough. That's about it, isn't
it?' and the old gentleman, having abandoned
his efforts after the reproduction of the appearance of a lemon awaiting the squeezer, leaned
forward and looked into his son's face with a
malicious grin.

Gideon was considerably taken aback at
this evidence of perfect knowledge on the part
of his parent of his monetary position. He
could not imagine how he had got to know so
much. Then he remembered it was part of his
father's stock-in-trade to keep machinery for
winnowing out the chaff from the corn when
the combination was presented to him by young
gentlemen desiring loans of money. He had

evidently had this at work with respect to his affairs.

'You are a regular sorcerer, father. It's no use trying to keep anything from you. If you know so much you will also know that my need is absolutely temporary, that I am more than solvent, and that I can afford to pay you good interest.'

'Yes, I know all that, and I know that things are even better than you think them. Within a year you'll begin to work off your mortgages, and be clear of them in five years with the property at increasing value. If you and me were in business together and knew of a case like yours wouldn't we like to get hold of him and sink him in loans, and then take over the speculation? I have thought it over myself. I knew you would come to me for help, and I did once think I would lend you money on our usual terms, then put on the screw and then draw off every acre of land you hold. But that would take time ; in the mean-

while you would get this election I know.　I
have been into that just as I have into your other
concerns, and you are quite sure to win.　Then
you would go into Parliament and have a nice
time of it, I suppose, before the screw began to
work.　But it would work in time and grind
you down, driving you out of the House and
out of the country.　That would be a neat bit
of vengeance, wouldn't it?　That would pay
you off for insulting your father, his house and
his business, rubbing his name off your door as
if it was a sign of the plague.'

The old gentleman was working himself up
into a violent passion, and Gideon began to
think things were not quite so promising as he
had imagined.

Suddenly the Spider stopped short, changed
his voice, and with it his whole aspect.　The
malicious leer gave place to a benevolent smile.
The fierce light in his eye died away into something like a twinkle.　And his harsh voice
became quite coaxing in its tone.　Gideon was

not unfamiliar with this transformation. He
had often seen his father look thus upon some
young sprig of nobility whose blood he was
sucking.

That reminiscence was not reassuring. Still
his father must have a heart. He had evidently
been thinking the matter over and could only
see it in one light. He was very faithful to his
family traditions, and what was Gideon doing
but raising the house on a new and more
glorious foundation ?

'Come, Ikey,' the old man continued in .a
soothing tone. 'Let us get to business. I
dare say you are going to church and perhaps
your carriage is waiting for you. How much
is it you want? and when would you like to
have the cash?'

Gideon was quite touched by this sudden
flash of affection breaking through the grim
exterior of the old gentleman's ill humour, a
natural ill humour Gideon felt bound to admit.
He had thwarted the old man's dearest hopes.

In a great measure he had done this unconsciously, particularly in what seemed to be the deepest stroke of all—the changing of his name. He would try and make it up with him now, and if he could only win over his father to see his prospects in the light he viewed them himself, they might all be happy yet, and, for even in this gush of natural sentimental affection Gideon was not insensible to the consideration, he would escape the danger he had feared of his father's willing his property away elsewhere.

. 'Well, father,' he said, gulping down something like a sob, 'I must say you're uncommonly good, much better than I expected or had any reason to hope for. It is a trifle for you and me, and, as you seem to know very well, I want it just to carry me over this election. I am nipped a bit with little expenses down at the place.'

'Little expenses!' the old gentleman repeated with a swift but happily only temporary fading out of the benevolent expression. 'Oh, well, we will call them little.'

Gideon saw he had made a mistake, and was still skating over thin ice.

'They are not so much expenses as investments out of which I shall get as much percentage as we used to make in Carlton Street. But what I want just now is 3,000*l.*'

'"Three thousand ducats," as the old gentleman says in the play where they heap abuse upon our race, despising them as much as some of us do our own birth and name. Three thousand ducats ! My ducats, my son, and my son's seat in Parliament, and his hobnobbing with dooks and elbowing of earls and canoodling with countesses. By the way, Ikey, why don't you ask some of your fine friends to lend you this money? The Dook of Wellington might have a trifle to spare, or the Duke of Morlbrer, or perhaps the Prince of Wales might lend it you on your note of hand.'

The Spider here went off in a fit of laughter,

in which the benevolence was burnt up, and
left him a snarling old man, looking at Gideon
with a malignant glance, which suggested that
if he had at the moment his heart's desire he
would stick a pin into him.

'You will have your joke, father; but you
have the best reason to know that dukes and
earls and their belongings are about the most
unlikely people in the world to have any spare
cash. I came to you, thinking first of all you
might like to help your son. Then I thought,
though you have retired from the business,
you wouldn't mind a little transaction where the
security was good and the interest not screwed
down.'

'Interest!' cried the old man, raising his
dirty hands with a gesture of horror. 'Take
interest from my own flesh and blood! Is it
possible that you could think so badly of your
old father?—though after what you have done
it's plain enough nothing's too bad for him in
your eyes. Not a penny interest will I take.

You shall have the cheque and no questions asked either about security or interest, or repayment. The time for that will rest with yourself. Now, I will write you the cheque.'

The Spider got up, and, skipping lightly across the room, produced from a small drawer an old envelope which had reached him through the post. He also brought over to the table pen and ink, the latter contained in one of the small stone bottles in which the fluid is dispensed by pennyworths. Laying the envelope on the table, he carefully cut off the flap side, and began to write on the other.

' I didn't get another cheque-book after using the last from Carlton Street,' he explained. ' I don't draw many cheques now, and what is the use of going and putting your money out to waste in stamps? Four and twopence for the smallest book; and suppose there was a fire in the place they might be burnt, and where's your remedy? Besides, I think the four and twopence is quite as safe in my pocket as in the Government's.'

He wrote slowly and carefully, the tallow candle lighting up with grim effect his eager shrivelled face and the grey unkempt hair, crowned by the black velvet skull-cap. Before he finished the benevolence had faded out of his face again, giving place to the earlier look of cruel maliciousness.

Doubtless this was due to the act of writing the cheque, naturally distasteful to him even when he had made up his mind to do a generous action.

' 'Aven't got a stamp in your pocket, have you, Ikey? I never carry them myself, but we must stamp the cheque.'

Gideon took out his pocket-book and handed a stamp to his father, who greedily licked it, stuck it on the sheet of paper, and wrote across in figures, as Gideon could see where he sat, ' 3,000*l*.'

' There you are,' he said, folding the docu-

·ment and handing it over to Gideon, 'and with your own receipt stamp, too. Now be happy; go and win your election, take your seat amongst the nobles of the land, and forget your old father.'

'Never!' cried Gideon, meaning it with all his heart. 'I have been very wrong and thoughtless, but I never meant all you thought I did in changing my name, and all that. I dare say we shall be able to make it up now. You will come down to Castle Fleyce, and see how proud I will be to show my father to my friends, and tell them how kind he always was to me, and is now, when I am in a hole.'

'Castle Fleyce!' the old gentleman shrieked, throwing himself back in his chair, and laughing in a way that had some of the melody of a hoarse crow. 'Castle Fleyce! Hee! hee! hee! But hadn't you better see the cheque's all right. Your father's getting a bit old now, and not so sharp in business matters as he used to be. He may have made it 5,000*l*.'

Gideon certainly would have liked to have looked at the cheque when it was handed to him, and was about instinctively to follow that impulse when the rush of genuine emotion, occasioned by his father's unexpected generosity, stopped him. He would not, even by so commonplace an action, suggest the necessity of checking off his father. He was putting the cheque away in his pocket-book, but, thus genially invited, he held it and read :—

'If the person calling himself Gideon Fleyce were starving in the gutter, and a pennyworth of bread would save his life, I would not give him a penny, much less Three Thousand Pounds.'

It was duly signed and, as Gideon had seen, the stamp put on the corner and over it written 3,000*l.*

The colour faded from Gideon's face as he read this infamous document, and a dangerous light came into his eyes as he turned them upon his father, who was sitting back in his arm-chair with his elbows on its supports, his chin resting on his hands. He was eyeing Gideon with the most intense delight, his lean body shaking with silent laughter.

'What does this mean?' said Gideon, lapsing straightway into the snuffling speech that betokened the profoundest depths of anger.

' It means,' cried the old man, springing up and speaking with the same snuffle, ' that you are a bigger fool than I took you for. What! you think you can thwart your father in his dearest hopes, insult and despise him, go your way, which certainly leads to destruction, and then when you are in a pickle you can come home and crawl round your father with the hope of wheedling him out of his hard-earned money? You are worse and more contemptible than I took you for. I did think you had some little sense. Bah! I hate and despise you, and renounce all kinship with you.'

And the old man spat at his son.

Gideon had not spoken a word since he asked the question, but stood with the same white face and set lip, looking steadily at the infuriated old man who in his rage danced about before him.

When this personal indignity was put upon him, he looked quickly round as if in search of something. If his stick had been upon the table it is possible that in the boundless passion that possessed him he might have sealed the family renunciation by knocking his father down. But there was nothing on the table save a knife.

Still in search for something handy, his eye fell upon the coal-scuttle almost filled with slack.

This he took up with both his hands, and before his father could quite realise the position half the contents were thrown over him.

The rest Gideon, not quite knowing what he did, flung on the fire and, violently pitching the coal-scuttle to the other end of the room, strode forth, pursued by his father, who, if the matter had not something tragical in it, would have looked ludicrous as he followed, spluttering and shaking his fist, alternately bewailing the loss of the precious fuel and calling on the God of Abraham, the God of Isaac, and the God of Jacob to curse this misbegotten son.

Before Gideon quite realised where he was he found himself walking at a tremendous pace westward up Fulham Road. He had taken the turning to the right, coming out of the street in which the bijou residence was situate, and blind with wrath had not noticed that he was walking in the wrong direction. The train he had proposed to return by left Charing Cross at ten o'olock. There was another at eight, and if on leaving his father's he had got into a cab and driven rapidly to the station he might have caught that and been home in good time.

It was too late to think of that now. The interview which he had reckoned on as pleasantly extending till it was time for him to leave to catch the ten o'clock train had come to an unexpectedly abrupt conclusion, and he had nearly a couple of hours on his hands.

The cool air and rapid walking had brought him down a little from the pitch to which he had risen when he sought solace in the coal-scuttle, and now there came back to him with fuller force the recollection that he had not got the money, and that the support on which he had been leaning with increasing confidence in its security had suddenly given way, and—this was an additional aggravation—had dropped him in the very moment when he thought he had succeeded.

When he recalled the cunning malignity his father had displayed, leading him up to the belief that he should have the money, and then heaping on him contumely and insult, his blood boiled again, his pulse beat fast, and his fist clenched. If he could hold something in it and strike his father, it would be a relief. The action of closing his hand and finding nothing in it reminded him of the stick.

He remembered how he had put it down in the corner at his father's bidding. It was a good stout stick, made out of an old hickory tree, cut down in the course of the alterations at the Castle. He had had a gold band put round it with his name on, 'Gideon Fleyce, Castle Fleyce,' and the date. Between his name and address was a blank space left, sufficient to fill in 'M.P.,' when the time should come.

He didn't like to lose the stick, and, above all, he hated the notion that it was in his father's possession. He knew what the old man would do with it. He would take off the gold rim, melt it down, and add it to his store of gold, which would be all the more precious to him since he would reflect that he had deprived his son of this morsel.

Gideon recalled the *finesse* with which the old gentleman got from him a receipt stamp wherewith to complete the delusion about the cheque. Even in full enjoyment of his revenge he would not spend a penny of his own money, and Gideon knew the fact that he had got this

pennyworth out of his son would multiply his
joy.

Gideon would have the stick, and perhaps
if he once got into the house again he might
find some way of getting the money. The old
gentleman had had his joke, and might, even at
the eleventh hour, relent. At any rate, it was
worth trying for. A drowning man wildly
looks round and clutches at a straw. He
would rather have a plank if there were one
about. But he clutches at what he can get,
and Gideon began to be glad that he had
accidentally left behind his stick, so that he
might have an excuse for returning. To be
near the treasure in the safe was something.

He turned round and walked back to the
bijou residence. Looking up it was as dark as
if Death, representing himself as a Bachelor of
Fortune, had secured the lease and taken up
his residence within the barred shutters and
down-drawn blinds. Gideon walked up and
down once or twice looking at the house and

watching for any sign of light or movement. Nothing came, as indeed it would have been strange if it had, seeing that a tallow dip, of which eighteen go to the pound, is not calculated to produce a light that would penetrate iron-bound shutters.

Gideon had once expressed surprise that his father, having all this cash so easily convertible, should dwell in the house by himself without having the fear of thieves before his eyes. But herein he did his father a fresh injustice. The old gentleman, if he had not been born and bred a usurer, would have made a living, and peradventure fame, as a mechanic. He was full of ingenious devices, and these he had worked out for his safety and the preservation of his property.

The bijou residence, in spite of its innocent appearance, was a sort of Trojan horse, introduced amongst unsuspecting houses of the vicinity. A burglar entering it, whether by door or window, would have been done to

death in various surprising but perfectly effec-
tual ways. The simplicity of the old gentleman was so remarkable that no one suspected
his infernal designs. When he opened the
front door he always just put the chain on, a
familiar device which the casual caller might
imagine was the full extent of his precautions.

An able-bodied burglar would have laughed
to scorn this old-fashioned precaution, and,
setting his shoulder against the door, would
have dragged the socket out of the staple.
Whereupon there would have fallen upon his
head or shoulder, according as he was more or
less advanced, a heavy steel blade fixed over
the doorway, and supported in its harmless
position by a cord attached to the socket in
which the door chain was ordinarily fastened.

This the Spider called his guillotine, and
was much attached to it. Other contrivances,
not quite so elaborate but equally efficacious,
defended the various shutters on the ground-
floor, while the door at the back of the house,

which gave out into a little yard, overshadowed by the backs of other houses, was practically a dummy. With the consciousness of these things bristling about in all directions the Spider might sit under his own vine and fig-tree, none daring to make him afraid.

Gideon, knowing nothing of these things, looked up and down the house, and reflected on the possibility of getting in, whether his father would let him or no. But first of all he would try the ordinary means of approach. He didn't doubt that after knocking at the door he would see once more through the aperture the wrinkled face, the velvet skull-cap, and the tallow candle held up aloft for the better illumination. Then he would, as before, put his foot inside the door and parley with his parent, leaving the rest to chance.

He had a good hour to spare, and might as well employ it in that way as in any other.

CHAPTER XXVI.

REHOBOTH.

REHOBOTH was not easy to find, even by the earnest seeker, unless he were furnished with very minute instructions. As Mr. Dumfy had incidentally mentioned to Gideon, the temple was situate in Camden Town. It stood in a busy street, but, as having little to do with things of this world, or with mundane affairs of any kind beyond the weekly offertory, it stood well back from the line of shops and houses.

On one side were the business premises of a coachbuilder, the proprietor's name and style being flaunted forth in gold letters standing upon a bright green ground. On the other was a tailor's shop, where, on Saturday nights, the gas flamed to its utmost. There were

large tickets on every article of dress displayed
in the window proclaiming its astonishing
cheapness, a common peculiarity being that
whatever might be the number of shillings de-
manded, the figure as to the pence was always
eleven. Moreover, whilst the shillings were
set forth in large letters, the elevenpence was
written so small that it was only on close in-
spection it could be discerned.

In fact it played on the price-card the part
which Rehoboth held towards the buildings in
the street. It was of supreme relative im-
portance; but of ineradicably retiring habits.

Another noticeable thing about the tailor's
shop was the never-failing presence of a gentleman dressed in the height of fashion, as fashion
was interpreted by Mr. Solomon, the tailor.
His clothes were running to seed, though this
was due, perhaps, not more to old age than to
constant exposure. When it actually rained
the walking gentleman went inside, like one of
the two figures in the barometer house, who,

when the weather is threatening, gives place to his brother made up for wet weather.

A marked peculiarity about this personage was that he never wore a head-piece. In the depth of winter, as in the height of summer, he appeared bareheaded, either walking up and down before the shop front, or standing at the door. He had cards in his hands setting forth the wonderful goodness and marvellous cheapness of the clothing to be purchased at Mr. Solomon's. If he saw any one who looked as if he would presently be wanting a suit of clothes he approached him, thrust a card in his hand, and seized the opportunity to make a few observations on the general quality of Mr. Solomon's stock-in-trade, and the advantageous terms on which it might be dealt with provided the present moment were seized.

Why he should thus perambulate the pavement before the premises without a hat was one of the mysteries of the trade. It might be thought that his recommendation of Mr.

Solomon's infallibly fitting coats and marvellously adapted trousers would have been equally efficacious if he had addressed the desired customer with his hat on. He might even have created a diversion by taking his hat off, and thus addressed the passer-by with outward marks of unwonted courtesy that might have been counted on to move him.

Somehow or other, at some time or other, in some place or other, there had been a man connected with the chief ready-made clothing establishment of the street who had stood at the door of his shop and made occasional excursions therefrom bareheaded. He had prospered exceedingly, and in the reckless way of generalising, which sometimes besets us, it appeared to some aspirant in the trade that the whole secret of his prosperity lay in the fact that he went out bareheaded.

Thus, doubtless, the practice sprang up, and in Camden Town and other parts of London, where cheap, ready-made clothing is in vogue, no establishment worth its salt is without its Bare-headed Man.

Mr. Solomon's bare-headed man was a shining light at Rehoboth. In fact—there need be no secret about it here—he was the proprietor of the place. Not finding it convenient or desirable it should be known that he was a moneyed man, Mr. Selth had originally set up as an agent for a mysterious proprietor, whose rents he received, and for whom he acted with plenary power. At the outset this arrangement had not been successful. Rehoboth had not proved a paying concern, and what funds were forthcoming had, as Mr. Selth held, been wrongly appropriated by the managing deacons.

Accordingly, when he found a new tenant, he took a fresh departure. He joined the church himself, was even elected deacon, and thus had direct control over the incomings, whilst his spiritual welfare was cared for on Sundays, he sitting practically pew-rent free.

Brother Selth approaching Rehoboth on the Sunday morning or Sunday evening was scarcely recognisable as the outdoor man of the flourishing cheap clothing establishment hard by. The change was largely due to his donning a hat on Sundays. It is astonishing what a difference it made in him.

Of course in ordinary life we get used to the change made in our acquaintances whom we meet sometimes in the house and occasionally in the street in the varied garb suited to the circumstances. But if we had a familiar friend, not being a Blue-coat boy, whom we were accustomed to see day after day, sun, rain, or snow, dressed for the street in every respect saving the wearing of a hat, it would not be without a shock that we should some day discover him crowned by the ordinary chimney-pot.

Brother Selth's hat looked new, which well it might, seeing it came out only fifty-two times in the year, and was carefully brushed and put away every week. To meet him walking up Camden Road with an umbrella in his hand and hat on his head was quite startling. On the other hand, there was something familiar about his aspect as he sat in his pew, clad in his overcoat, devoutly taking part in the service of the chapel, and, of course, with his hat off.

It was a further peculiarity of this remarkable man that on Sundays he not only wore a hat but carried an umbrella, wet or fine ; and lastly, summer or winter, he wore his overcoat on a Sunday, sitting with it closely buttoned up throughout the service, even though the thermometer might be eighty degrees in the shade.

Under its new aspect Rehoboth was going on in a moderately prosperous way. The Rev. Josiah Waffle had proved a great attraction. The chapel filled, the seat-rents were all paid, and the offertory, though not quite coming up to that of Mr. Spurgeon's Tabernacle, for example, was a promising and improving feature.

After some of his sermons, in which Mr. Waffle had been able to paint the hereafter of other people in exceptionally dismal colours, there was cast up as much as 9*s.* 7*d.* in the boxes at the door. Last Sunday, as the label above the box testified, there had only been 3*s.* 3*d.*, a circumstance which, taken in conjunction with what we know of an early conversation Mr. Dumfy held with his employer, incontestably proved that that gentleman had not been in his place on the previous Sabbath.

This was the fact ; but Mr. Dumfy was in his place now, and the blood in the veins of Rehoboth seemed to move with quickened life. Although Brother Selth was senior deacon, and by virtue of that office sat at the little desk underneath the pulpit from which the Rev. Mr. Waffle liberally dispensed damnation, he always made a point of retiring in favour of Mr. Dumfy, when that personage was present.

Taking it as a whole, the congregation at Rehoboth was richer in spiritual grace than in worldly goods. Mr. Dumfy, as the confidential clerk of an eminent financier, was a triton among these minnows. He was generally understood to be a ' warm ' man, and if there was any condition that was exceptionally attractive to Brother Selth it was that a brother or a sister should be ' warm ' in the sense that somewhere or other he or she had large possessions.

In respect of this belief affecting Brother Dumfy, Brother Selth and the rest of the congregation walked by faith. If Brother Dumfy were wealthy he was careful to hide all proof thereof, doubtless not wishing to vaunt his riches in the eyes of brethren whom Providence had not blessed in equal measure. Even that little extra weekly payment he had secured from Gideon on the alleged account of Rehoboth was dispensed in secret, and, strange to say, without any appreciable effect on the weekly collection, which sometimes fell below three shillings.

It was characteristic of Brother Selth, who managed this part of the business, that when he made up the slip of paper that was stuck from Sunday to Sunday over the offertory box, proclaiming the amount collected on the previous Sabbath, he always made provision for three denominations of coin.   From Sunday to Sunday £. *s. d.* stared the congregation in the face, the £. bearing up bravely against its unrelieved desolation, and taking no note of the fact that the weeks passed and resembled each other to the extent that after the £ there was always a dash, intimating that the amount last week had not run to sovereigns.

But who should say what might happen? At any rate Brother Selth would be on the safe side, ranging the full extent of the monetary alphabet.   Besides, it was likely to have a good effect upon the congregation, bringing constantly before them the fact that in diaconal circles it was regarded as by no means outside the range of reasonable expectation that some week or other they might run the amount of the offertory over twenty shillings.

Brother Dumfy's business was to give out the hymns, reading them verse by verse, after which the words were taken up by the tuneful choir. Just now the Rev. Mr. Waffle was reading and expounding one of the lessons. The exposition stood towards the text in the relation which Falstaff's mixture of sack held towards the complement of bread. Mr. Waffle was evidently of opinion that the older apostles were all very well in their way, but it would be better for a congregation living in these happy times to have a great deal of Waffle, and very little of Paul.

So he read a few lines from Paul, apostle to the Church at Ephesus, and interpolated long passages from Josiah, apostle to the Church named Rehoboth.

This interlude gave Brother Dumfy an opportunity to gaze round the chapel, in which he had not lately been, owing to pressure of affairs at Saxton. It was a very small place, and when filled did not hold more than one hundred and fifty people. Brother Selth had bought it cheap, the former landlord falling into difficulties in respect of rates. Being a man of taste, he had ' done it up,' painting the walls a lively maroon colour, that being a shade warranted to wear well and conceal the marks of hands and heads, and had lavishly illuminated the windows above the pulpit with a few panes of purple-stained glass, which made a nice contrast with the paint on the walls.

Standing well back from the line of shops, Rehoboth was approached by a gravelled walk running between a grass plot, on which there grew here and there a few straggling blades of grass, which came up very black in the face, and early displayed predisposition towards withering. Half a dozen trees which had reached a good height attested the comparative antiquity of the chapel. In the early spring the trees diffidently put forth a few leaves, wonderfully green and tender-looking. But they did not live long, nor grow beyond their dwarfed estate. Ivy had been planted by the wall of Mr. Solomon's cheap and ready-made clothing establishment. But ivy, which will grow almost anywhere in London, did not come to much in this gloomy passage. It had assimilated soot in quite a phenomenal manner, and very early in the spring the young leaves, as they came forth, went into mourning for each other, and presently the short and doleful spell of their lives was over.

Perhaps if you heard the Rev. Mr. Waffle, as he preached his sermon, you might have gained some inkling of the reason why the trees and grass and ivy should be thus blighted. Mr. Waffle had very decided views on the ultimate destination of people outside the walls of Rehoboth. There had never been any hope for them from the first, and this Sabbath, even more than a week ago, they were hastening with quickened footsteps to the brink of the bottomless pit, into which they would surely fall with shrieks and wails, which Mr. Waffle sometimes imitated for the edification of his congregation.

His sermon was, to tell the truth, one suffocating whiff of fire and brimstone, and this, passing out through the open chapel doors in summer time, or stealing through the crevices of door and window in winter, could not fail to have its effect upon the innocent herbage and the struggling leaves on the soot-begrimed trees.

But the congregation liked it, and Brother Selth particularly approved it, since it kept the chapel unprecedentedly full.

If Mr. Waffle was right, and a man who perspired so freely, and who so little spared the pulpit cushion, could not be otherwise than right, heaven was to be found only *vià* the walls of Rehoboth. Therefore Rehoboth in these times rarely had more than a dozen seats unlet.

Everything was plain about Rehoboth, especially the woman kind. Mr. Waffle himself was no beauty, rather running to cheek-bone, with pallid face, abundance of unkempt black hair, and a pair of glistening eyes that flashed terribly as he discoursed on the sins of others and the certainty of retribution. Mr. Waffle 'enjoyed bad health,' as the chapel-keeper said, with something of pardonable pride, and as he stood up in the old deal pulpit, fashioned something after the shape of a coffin with the broad end uppermost, he suggested uncanny thoughts to the imaginative. That is, he might have carried such suggestion if imagination had formed any part of the attributes of his listeners.

But that was doubtful. They were good plain people, who worked hard through the week, and liked to take their religion strong on Sundays. The men were for the most part dull-looking, and the peace and rest of the Sabbath was evidently handicapped for them by the awkward consciousness of being in their Sunday clothes. The women were decidedly dowdy in appearance, the majority dressed in rusty black. Here and there was a backslider who illuminated the dead level with patches of blue or purple or brick red, displayed in bonnet or shawl. These were the objects of much wrestling in prayer and many conversations over the tea-tables by the elder women.

All told, there were but five of these worldlings. Priscilla Ann Twentyman, the one in the light blue bonnet with neckshawl of purple-hued wool, was 'engaged.' But no one could say when the engagement would find its legitimate issue in matrimony. Sister Twentyman, Priscilla's mother, was an obstacle in the way. 'The young man,' Brother Doke, was present in chapel on this particular Sabbath; but, as usual, Sister Twentyman interposed her angular body between the two lovers.

Brother Doke was a mild young man not given to asserting his rights. He had now been engaged for seven years, and was willing to marry. Sister Twentyman always whined when the subject was mentioned, as if she had received a personal injury. She spoke at length, though in a broken voice, of the ingratitude of children, and so worked upon the feelings of the unfortunate young man that he was glad to retire into private where he could abuse himself for his lack of considerateness and all good feeling.

There were some who said that Priscilla never would be married. Certainly she got every winter more and more to resemble her mother in appearance, temper, and even voice. But Brother Doke did not take note of any of these things. He was there to be married whenever it was quite convenient to other parties, and in the meantime he took Sister Twentyman out to penny readings, cheap concerts, and morning and evening service at Rehoboth. On these occasions Priscilla had accidentally, but invariably, sat on the other side of her mother, and the old lady became the unconscious conductor of many heart-throbs that passed between the hapless couple.

Alas, poor, pallid Priscilla, and dumb devoted Doke! If you only had the courage some fine morning to lock in the upper chamber this ogress that tramples on your timid love, and makes a profit in the shape of votive offerings and tickets for tea-parties out of your respect for Priscilla's mother, and were thereafter straightway to hie thee to church or chapel, where you might be swiftly married, all would be well. There would be some tearfulness when you returned, unlocked the door, and made a clean breast of your crime. The ogress would see as in a flash of lightning how her opportunity was gone; for there is a wide difference even in so simple a mind as that of Brother Doke's between a mother-in-law and the mother of her with whom you 'keep company.' No more votive offerings in the shape of new caps with gorgeous ribbons. No more gloves, black and a size too large for convenience in pulling on. No more wild moments at the Polytechnic, nor any more debauches at Panoramas of the Holy Land with nuts and oranges, and, peradventure, ever so small a drop of gin brought in a case bottle and dispensed on returning home, perhaps not without a view to certainty of invitation to enter if it be known that the flask is in the pocket.

All this the mother of Priscilla would see. But it would be no use kicking against the pricks, and thenceforward Brother Doke might become as much master of the situation as was possible to one of his retiring habits But it is not likely that this *coup d'état* will ever disturb the serenity of the household, and many years may pass before these mildewed lives are freed from the influence that blights them.

The gods don't love Priscilla's mother, and she is likely to live to be very old.

It was known to the elders of the congregation that Brother Dumfy on this particular night would not be able to stay out the full measure of the service. He had run up to town, at great personal expense and much inconvenience, to share in the privilege of worship at Rehoboth. He must needs return by the eight o'clock train, business of this world peremptorily calling him back to Saxton. He would sit in his old place at the little red-cushioned desk underneath the coffin-shaped pulpit, and go through the service up to the threshold of the sermon. Then he would retire, and Brother Selth, walking boldly up with his hymnbook held in his right hand as if it were one of the cards attesting the immense advantages of Mr. Solomon's establishment, would take the vacant seat. In the meantime Brother Dumfy had two hymns to give out, and this he did with much unction.

Of course there was at Rehoboth no trifling with Belial in the shape of a harmonium. Even a tuning-fork was dispensed with, everything in the musical line resting with Brother Psyder, who, unaided by any other gift than the vocal one with which an inscrutable Providence had endowed him, led the tuneful choir.

Brother Psyder sat in the background under the shade of the coffin, and it was not till Brother Dumfy had read out the first verse that he came forward, and, laying his open tune-book on his brother's desk, leaned his right arm thereupon, and, with his hymnbook held close to his eyes, raised the tune.

Throughout the week Brother Psyder was in a small way of business in the butter, cheese, and bacon line. He was volatile enough when behind the counter, hopping here and there to meet the varied demands of ready-money customers. But on Sundays he was wont to assume an expression of stolidity, understood to be appropriate to his responsible position. When standing in full view of the congregation, pausing a moment before filling the dumb chapel with melody, the result of his efforts to assume a devotional aspect was to convey to his face the appearance of having been carved out of a turnip. It was absolutely expression-less, and with great skill was kept so through-out the singing of the hymn.

Brother Psyder, whose face was otherwise bare, cultivated a little goatee beard, which played an important part in his ministrations. By long practice he had achieved the art of singing without opening his mouth beyond the slightest appearance of a crack, nor did he in any degree visible to the congregation move his lips. But the action of the goatee beard bore testimony to the physical effort, and gave an appearance of mobility to his countenance otherwise lacking.

It was surprising, considering the size of the aperture, what tremendous sounds Brother Psyder was able to emit through this crack. He had evidently devoted a good deal of thought to the avocation, and had evolved a practice which presented his special gifts in the strongest light. It was his habit to sing the first two lines of the verse at the loudest pitch of his stentorian voice. Then the thunder ceased, and there played through the building the soft lightning of female voices.

This was 'forty and peeaner,' as Brother Psyder explained to the church meeting at which the matter was discussed, after the first experiment. The explanation was accepted as satisfactory, and the style of singing thenceforward was formally accepted at Rehoboth. Brother Selth was inclined to think it worthily seconded the efforts of the Rev. Mr. Waffle to keep the pews occupied.

Whether Brother Psyder himself took part in the piano movement always remained a matter for controversy. But since, whilst this part of the verse was being sung his eyebrows were observed to be uplifted, and the goatee was clearly seen to move up and down with gentle motion, there is reason to believe that at this stage he sang falsetto.

Brother Dumfy might have solved the

mystery if he had had time to turn his thoughts to it. Brother Psyder leaned upon his desk as he sung, and may be said to have warbled in his ear. But Brother Dumfy's thoughts were occupied with other things.

This was the occasion of his fortnightly visit to town, and he was ordinarily accustomed to remain all night, and return to Saxton in the course of Monday. To-day, pleading the exigencies of the election, he had made it known that he must positively go down to Saxton by the eight train. He had been at the morning service, and would not miss what measure was possible of the evening exercise. He would sit in his place in full view of his brothers and sisters, with the tuneful Psyder on his left, and the energetic Waffle in the box above him. When the time came he would slip out, pick up the small black bag he had deposited in the vestry, and wend his way to Charing Cross. He had already taken an affectionate leave of Mrs. Dumfy, who was now in the family pew, and proposed to herself to enjoy to the full the ministrations of the place.

Brother Dumfy had occasion to think kindly of Saxton and of events there. Since Gideon had blundered into his encounter with Long Bill on the subject of the expenditure on the flagstaff, he had refrained from interfering with Brother Dumfy's petty cash, which more and more displayed an adhesive tendency as it passed through the fingers of its custodian.

But whilst there is a silver lining to every cloud, so boundaries of black edge off every patch of blue sky, whether broad or narrow. Brother Dumfy shared, with honest indignation, the grievance of the 'Longshore men that the election was being hurried forward in a highly reprehensible manner. Before the Sabbath had twice returned all would be over, accounts would be squared up, and he knew sufficient of Gideon's nature to foresee that after this burst of lavish expenditure there would come a period of excessive economy, and a season of prying into the disposition of petty cash.

Brother Dumfy's appetite had grown with what it fed upon. He had made a good thing out of recent opportunities, but he felt he would like, if possible, to get one great haul before opportunity was dead. He was, as was bruited about in the chapel, a warm man, much warmer than even the wildest fancy pictured, warmer even than Brother Selth, although he took high rank as the proprietor of Rehoboth. But if this was being warm, Brother Dumfy felt he would like to be hot, and he had often turned over in his mind schemes for reaching that happy condition.

However, what he had now to do was to get back to Saxton, and when the Rev. Mr. Waffle laid his open book on the uncushioned desk of the pulpit, and gave a thump preparatory to announcing his text, Brother Dumfy, momentarily drooping his head on his hands to hide the eyes that were homes of silent prayer, stole away with long stride and soft footfall towards the vestry, where his small handbag lay, and near it his faithful weather-worn umbrella.

Though easily portable, the bag was a good deep one, made of cowhide, and certainly big enough to hold Brother Dumfy's thick woollen 'comforter.' It seemed a strange way to carry a neck covering. But we all have odd personal habits. Opening the bag, Brother Dumfy took out the comforter, and, after a moment's hesitation as to whether he should put it on now or wait until he got into the train, returned it to the bag. Perhaps when he came to close the bag and carry it from the vestry in his hand, the foolishness of thus lumbering himself with useless luggage may have struck him.

There was in the vestry a small washstand which shut up within its case, and which Brother Selth had bought cheap at a sale. In the lid was set a bit of looking-glass, and Brother Dumfy, turning this up, produced from his coat pocket a small comb and brush, and carefully attended to his curls. Then, taking his bag in one hand and the umbrella in the other, he went out into the street by the vestry door.

As he walked down Hampstead Road with intent to get the 'bus that passed Charing Cross, he might have felt, if there had been anything like pride about him, that Camden Town did not contain any more highly respectable-looking man. The critical observer might have taken exception to a trifle of spottiness about his hat, and the edge of his trousers were just a trifle frayed at the heel. But these, while indicative of honest poverty, were not conflicting with utter respectability, whilst the closely buttoned morning coat he wore left little to be desired, betraying even a stylishness of cut that gave the wearer (for a deacon) quite a jaunty air.

'Poor but honest,' was Brother Dumfy's own description of himself, and, as he deferentially took his seat in the 'bus dimly lighted from the oil lamp over the door, that would have been precisely the description applied to him by a casual observer.

At Charing Cross Brother Dumfy had a little time to spare, and, seeing that by the bounty of Gideon he possessed a season ticket, he might have sat through a portion of the Waffle discourse and still have caught his train. But he always liked to be in time. Though there was yet a quarter of an hour to spare, the train was drawn up at the siding, and Brother Dumfy, leisurely walking down the platform, found a carriage that had evidently been partially appropriated, for it held the baggage of at least two passengers. He took his seat with his back to the engine, and very near indeed to the engine, for he had hit upon the first carriage.

After a few minutes the other passengers arrived and took their seats. There were yet six minutes to spare, and Brother Dumfy, finding the prospect of an hour and a half's journey before him, thought he might as well stretch his legs. There was no need to take his umbrella with him, and no fear of any one, unless it was a collector of curiosities, stealing it. It was a good, honest, antiquated, green gingham, with a metal handle cast in the shape of a dog's head, and was probably as old as her gracious Majesty. But the bag Brother Dumfy would not leave, albeit it contained only a woollen comforter. So taking it with him he went for a stroll on the platform.

It was well he did not go far, for the train was punctual to a moment, and as the hand of the clock pointed to the figure eight it steamed out of the station and away into the dark night, past the little towns and villages with their twinkling lights, and through the fields on which the ghostly white mist hung low.

CHAPTER XXVII.

THE MARSHES AND THE MOAN OF THE SEA.

MIDNIGHT was striking as Gideon quickly issued from the carriage that brought him down to the junction. He did not want to be seen by the police station-master or the deferential porters, who might know him as the rich and popular candidate for Saxton, lavish with tips. So he slipped out into the road, and made at the top of his speed in the direction of Saxton. He had had a very bad day all together, and was physically, as well as mentally, upset by something he had seen on the line coming down from London.

A fearful accident, memorable in the annals of railway disaster, had happened, and Gideon had come almost in contact with some of the bodies of the victims.

The train leaving Charing Cross two hours earlier than the one he travelled by had fallen upon grievous mishap when thirty miles on its way. At this portion of the road the line ascended with a somewhat steep incline for the distance of nearly two miles. A luggage train had preceded the eight o'clock train, and if all had gone well was to have shunted at Ashham to allow the passenger train to go its way. But just before arriving at Ashham the coupling chain had broken midway in the luggage train, and half the waggons having overcome the forward impetus, first of all stood still, then moved backwards at a pace the velocity of which increased at every yard. Before they had gone a mile they were travelling at the rate of thirty miles an hour, and still increasing their pace.

The passenger train meanwhile dashed along with perfect confidence, induced by the assumption that the line was clear at least as far as Ashham. When it had breasted the incline for a little over a quarter of a mile the paralysed engine-driver discovered sweeping down round the curve the five heavily laden waggons. He reversed the engine, and, having done all that was possible, he and his mate jumped off just before the shock came.

It came nevertheless with a tremendous force. The engine leaped like a mad living thing on top of the foremost waggon, burying itself amidst the wreck of the waggon beyond It is probable the shock of the fearful collisioi instantly killed the occupants in the carriages of the passenger train nearest the engine. It would be well to think so, since otherwise a more fearful fate than death by dislocation of the neck or fracture of the ribs awaited them.

The waggons were loaded with petroleum oil, and the barrels bursting open in the shock dashed their contents over the engine, and far down the line of carriages. The engine fire caught the inflammable substance, and in a moment the whole of the front part of the train was wrapt in fierce flames.

The fire was put out, and the charred remains had been collected in a heap and decently covered before the mail train by which Gideon travelled arrived at the spot. But the scene told too graphically what had happened, and Gideon, his nervous state increased by the worry of the day and the fact that scarcely any food had passed his lips, fancied he could smell burning flesh, from which he shrank with almost hysterical terror.

Arrangements had been made to prevent the delay of the mail train as much as possible. A train had been sent up from the coast terminus, and the passengers of the mail were conducted, with a little under half an hour's delay, from one train to the other, and so pursued their journey.

Gideon nearly lost his passage, being found huddled up in the corner of a carriage, which he had had all to himself from Charing Cross. The guard and the porter helped him round past the wreck of the broken and burnt train, and past a mound which, as they skirted it, looked like a heap of rubbish with tarpauling spread over it.

Gideon knew instinctively that there lay the victims of the tragedy, and he cowered in such abject terror that the guard and porter, each putting a stalwart arm round him, carried him into the train waiting on the other side. Here some one gave him a drink of brandy, which he hastily swallowed, and was well enough not only to pursue his journey, but when he arrived at the junction to get out and set forth on his lonely walk to Saxton.

The night was not always dark. There were thick clouds in the sky, but there was also a wild wind overhead, which swept them onward after a fashion that gave the moon many chances. It was nearly full moon, and the light that shines by night would have done very well if left to itself, as it testified whenever it got a chance of appearing in patches of the clear sky. Then fields and roads were flooded in the bright light. But presently up came a bank of dark cloud, and Gideon was floundering along through the muddy roads in almost total darkness.

It was a cold night, but he did not seem to notice it, or indeed to be aware of the quickly succeeding changes of light and darkness. He knew the road pretty well, having often driven along it. In any case it was not difficult to follow. Having once set his face towards Saxton there was no danger of going astray, since the highway was a long lane that had no turning till it reached the top of the hill from which the lights of Saxton, at such early hours as it had lights to show, might be seen twinkling below.

There was a sign-post at the four cross roads, one of which led by a steep descent to the marshes, beyond the loneliness of which

moaned the sea.   Gideon had never been down
there, but he had looked out on the great
waste sometimes, and had shuddered when he
thought what it would be on a dark, cold night,
for one who wandered there without friends
and without hope in the world.   He was not an
imaginative man, and when he had looked out
on the marshes he had shuddered simply with
that feeling with which prosperous plumpness
revolts from anything physically unpleasant.

It was Napper, who had in a few words
drawn the picture of the hopeless man stumb-
ling on amid this loneliness, looking out herself
the while with troubled, tearful eyes, as if she
could see the despairing wretch, and acutely
felt her helplessness to rescue him.

Gideon had at the time thought it would
be uncommonly unpleasant, wet to the feet,
and ruinous to the nether garments.   And
then supposing after wandering about all night
he escaped tumbling into the sea, or getting up
to the armpits in slush, he must needs lie down

And what a horrible mess his clothes would be in from head to foot !

As Gideon walked rapidly along in the middle of the road with his hat thrust back on his head and the moonlight falling on his face, he would scarcely have been recognised in Saxton. All the pleasant, rosy plumpness of the man seemed to have withered at a touch. He looked older and haggard. His lips were drawn down and his eyes burned with quite unwonted brilliancy. If the doctor had felt his pulse, and held his hot hand in his own for a moment, he would have said he was on the verge of an attack of fever.

Gideon was not in a humour to analyse his own feelings. All he knew was that hitherto life had been very pleasant with him and increasingly prosperous. Everything had gone well, and he had had no care beyond anxiety as to the fit of a coat or the sustained brilliancy of the nap of his hat. Now, in a moment, in the twinkling of an eye, the whole thing had changed. The sun had gone down, and black night covered the earth.

He cursed himself for his stupidity in allowing things to run their own course uncontrolled for so long a time. If he had spent a few hundreds less; if he had not paid cash when bills would have been equally acceptable, or if he had recognised the imminence of ruin before ruin had gathered all its forces and threatened to topple over and crush him, he would not be as he was at that moment. Things were worse then than they had been at this time yesterday, and they would be worse still at this time to-morrow. He was not a penny richer now than he had been when he started for London in the morning, and he was by so many hours nearer the crisis.

It did him good to curse himself, rousing him from the stupor into which he had fallen, partly under the influence of the unaccustomed brandy, and partly because he was dead beat.

When he reached the four cross roads at

the top of the hill he stopped and looked away to the right, down the dark lane at the end of which he knew the marshes were, and beyond them the sea. The wind was blowing inland, and he could hear the low thunder of the surf upon the shore. He was thoroughly wretched in mind and body, and there came to him a soothing sense of the ineffable peace and rest that was to be had down in the marshes. In his fevered state, with his stomach empty, his heart full, and his mind disordered, he saw nothing but shame and defeat in the coming days. He who had been accustomed to play Napoleon would be scoffed at as an adventurer who had failed.

Much of this was a fevered fantasy. Things were not so bad as they seemed regarded from the gloomy depths of Gideon's mind. He was not accustomed to being crossed, and had gone down at the first stroke of ill-fortune. He might still get the 3,000*l.* ; but if he didn't, what would be the worst? He would certainly lose his election, but his land schemes were as sound now as they had been at any time. A little retrenchment in his personal expenses, a little patience, and a little assistance, which many people were interested in furnishing, would put him all right.

This is perhaps how Gideon might have seen the matter if he had gone home, gone to bed, had a long sleep, and lived till the morning. But whilst it is all very well for us, discussing these things from our comfortable chairs, and out of the profundity of our orderly, well-spent lives, it was different to Gideon standing alone by the finger-post on this wild March night, with the clouds above him scudding past as if they too were glad to get clear of a man whom fortune had deserted.

Gideon's fancy, taking a fresh turn, pictured the finger-post as a gallows, and he shrank affrighted from underneath the extended beam where he had been standing. There came back to him the thought of the dinner-party which

O'Brien was supposed to give, and the judge's description of his brother on the bench who was so fond of hanging people. He struggled desperately against this thought, which was not pleasant company in the circumstances. But it constantly returned, and would not be dismissed.

He walked away from the finger-post and stood irresolutely at the head of the road leading to Saxton. Still on his right hand was the lane leading down to the marshes, with the soothing sound of muffled thunder beyond. What a deal of trouble he would have been saved if he had only caught the eight o'clock train! What he feared most was that people would turn against him, and speak ill of him as a man who had failed. He liked to walk about with his head held up and to think people were saying,

'There goes Gideon Fleyce, an immensely wealthy man, who made his money by a grand *coup* in land, got into Parliament, and is hand-and-glove with all the big-wigs.'

The means by which this was to be accomplished formed a consideration that did not
greatly trouble him. Of course the thing
should be done by legitimate business, and above
all by keeping inside the pale of the law.
But Gideon knew well enough that when a
man is as successful as he had counted upon
being, the world would not too closely question
the source of his money-getting. He yearned
for success and prosperity, of both of which he
had hitherto enjoyed his full share. It was an
atmosphere in which he blossomed, and in
which, more especially under the guidance of
Napper, quite unexpected good qualities had
begun to sprout.

Now he felt all was over, and within a week
he would have to leave Saxton, abandon Castle
Fleyce, and go back to his dim life in Carlton
Street. Anything was better than that. If he
had only caught the eight o'clock train the
matter would have been settled without his
raising a finger to hasten its conclusion. It

could not be very pleasant to be burnt to cinders in a railway accident. But as he found himself arguing with strange minuteness and keen personal interest, the passengers must have been killed first or rendered insensible by the shock, and of what happened afterwards they neither knew nor felt anything.

If he went down to the marshes it would not be greatly different. People would suppose he had lost his way, and perhaps might, as they would have done in the case of a railway accident, say what a pity it was that such a brilliant career was thus cut short by a fatal accident. All the country would ring with his name, and no one would know how he actually stood on the brink of failure.

And how tired he was, and how sick at heart, and how petulantly impatient with the laws of life!

On the other hand, there were the long hours that must elapse before the end came, the hateful slush, the marrow-piercing cold, the darkness, the loneliness, and perhaps, after all, the failure in this too. He had his star like Napoleon. He thought it would blaze over the Austerlitz of his election to Parliament. But that was over, and, if he even tried to make an end of himself and his troubles, he would surely fail again.

There flashed before his mind the picture of a crowd of people carrying into Castle Fleyce the insensible form of a man covered with mud ('Just as if I had fallen down drunk,' he said to himself), who should be put to bed and brought to with restoratives in time to learn that all was over with his great schemes, that the election had been lost, and the mortgagees had foreclosed.

This settled the controversy in his mind. If he was going to do anything it should not be in that way. He turned and walked rapidly down the hill in the direction of Castle Fleyce. There was nobody about, and no chance of his being seen. He would get back through the shrubbery and into the study without any one being the wiser. Then if he pleased he might go out of the world in a gentleman-like way with a pistol at his head.

Though—again arguing it out in the oddly logical way in which he had discussed things at the finger-post—that would be a very different thing from taking the wrong turning, losing his way among the marshes, being found after many days, and brought home amid every manifestation of sorrow and respect for a man whose promising career had been thus tragically cut short. To commit suicide would be the most successful way in the world to advertise his failure, and would not do any good beyond gratifying his momentary passion for the rest of oblivion. He would go to bed now, and perhaps sleep on it.

As he approached within a mile of Castle Fleyce he saw down the road a figure which struck him as being familiar, and which as it drew a few paces nearer he recognised.

It was Mr. Tandy, with his hands behind his back, strolling up the road. This was not a habit of that gentleman, nor it had not been one for many years. When he was a younger man, and was sometimes borne down by the pressure of overwork, he would break out into the country in the coolness and stillness of the night, a roving tendency which probably found its hereditary development in Napper's long country excursions, though these, as better befitted a young lady, were accomplished in the daytime.

On this particular Sunday Mr. Tandy had recurred to the earlier habit. He was tired and in low spirits, the combined result of his enduring exertions in Gideon's behalf and of Napper's estrangement. When Napper had kissed him and gone to bed Mr. Tandy had sat by the fire an hour thinking over many things. Then he had got up meaning to go to bed. Suddenly there came upon him a desire to go out into the cool night air and the darkness.

So he buttoned up his coat, whistled to Knut and went forth, walking slowly and thinking deeply.

Knut saw the stranger in the distance before Mr. Tandy, and it was the rigid attitude of attention assumed by the dog that caused his master to lift his eyes and look along the road. At first it struck him that this was Gideon ; but he dismissed the idea as impossible. The man was standing still in the broad moonlight. Mr. Tandy could even see that he had his hat well back on his head, and that his trousers were turned up almost to the knee.

'It's some tramp,' he said to himself, and took a firmer hold of his stick.

As he looked he beheld the stranger suddenly scale the gate against which he stood and disappear behind the hedge.

As an officer of the law, a resident in Saxton, and a householder himself, Mr. Tandy thought this was a thing to be looked into. Quickening his pace and sending Knut on before him, he got up to the gate just in time to see the man skulking along by the hedge in the direction of the plantation which skirted it on the other side, and gave access to Castle Fleyce.

'Hallo!' he shouted; but the man made no answer, except such as was conveyed by boldly leaving the shadow of the hedge and taking to his heels across the field.

Gideon thought he could reach the plantation before Mr. Tandy could get up to him. Once there he would make his way into the house and be comfortably seated in his study, supposing this meddlesome old fool were to go the length of knocking up the household with reports of a strange man lurking about the premises.

But he had counted without Knut. Mr. Tandy seeing the man throw off all disguise and bolt, was convinced either that he was bent upon evil, or that he had done evil. In either case he felt it his duty to secure him.

'Hi! Knut,' he cried, pointing to the re ceding figure of the proprietor of Castle Fleyce desperately making for his stronghold, ' after him !'

At the word Knut bounded off, and Gideon hearing his cry and looking back saw the dog galloping over the short grass. In two minutes he would be upon him. It was too ridiculous to be fighting with the dog of his legal agent, and besides, the consequences might be unplea- sant. Gideon had a vague notion that dogs of any kind invariably flew at one's throat. At best he knew that Knut would hold him, by what ever convenient place he managed to set his teeth in, till his master came up.

'Lie down ! Good old dog, lie down !' he said, turning and facing Knut, who, recognising his voice and perceiving there must be some mistake, abandoned his earlier purpose, and, turning back, proceeded slowly and with a dejected air to acquaint his master.

It was undoubtedly a great disappointment

to the dog. The chevying of sheep was for-
bidden to him under heavy penalties, the great-
est of all being the loss of Napper's favour.
Here had something come to him quite unexpectedly, and, as he might have said had he
been a French poodle, *pour combler de bonheur*.
For just when he was thinking of turning in to
his lonely couch on the mat at the foot of the
stairs, his master, in a never-before-remem-
bered way, had started up and proposed a
walk.

Knut would hardly believe his senses when
they realised what was in store for him. After
having thoroughly enjoyed the out, running
backwards and forwards, and making five miles
for every one covered by his master, his super-
lative benefactor, with an agility far beyond his
years, climbs a gate, takes him into a field,
shows him a man, and not only permits him to
chevy him, but commands him to do so. And
then after all that the man should turn out to
be Gideon Fleyce, the proprietor of the neigh-

bouring castle, the prospective member of Parliament for the borough, and, worse than all in the present circumstances, a person whom he had seen in his master's house evidently on friendly terms, and one whom Napper frequently talked to!

No wonder that Knut, walking back to rejoin his master, drooped his head and flung back his ears, whilst the bushy tail, wont on the slightest occasion to wave its flossy fringe ecstatically, now hung despondingly.

'Is that you, Tandy?' Gideon shouted. 'What the deuce do you mean by setting your dog on me? I thought you were some tramp.'

'Mr. Fleyce!' Mr. Tandy cried. 'God bless my soul! What an odd thing; I thought *you* were a tramp.'

'Well, I have been on the tramp,' said Gideon, determined to put a pleasant face on an awkward incident. 'I didn't feel inclined to go to bed, and after supper turned out for a bit of a stroll.'

'So did I.   Precisely my case ; only I am afraid I gave you a bit of a start,' he added, looking anxiously at Gideon's pale face, ghastly in the moonlight, and his disordered clothes, his boots covered with mud, and his trousers splashed to the knees.   'You look quite scared.   And no wonder !   I should have been the same myself to have a man chasing me with a dog.   Only when you got over the gate, and made for the Castle, I thought you were up to no good.'

'You are very kind to look after us by night as well as by day.   This is a near cut to the Castle.   I was just turning in, and now I will say good-night.'

'Shall I walk with you ? '

'No, I know my way.'

But it seemed that if he had at any time known it he had now forgotten it.   Getting into the plantation he hurriedly and vaguely felt his way, thinking he was making for the Castle. Presently he discovered he was skirting the road, and a dash to the left brought him out at the back of the Castle. There was no danger of his being seen, and getting on the turf he made his way round to the study window. This he opened without difficulty, and found the room apparently as he had left it, with the chicken and claret on the table.

If he had not been so tired and exhausted he would have noticed that there was a bright fire burning in the hearth, which seemed strange considering no one had been in since he left in the afternoon.

Gideon drank a tumbler of claret, ate a bit of bread, and toyed with a slice of the fowl, but he had no appetite, and felt he should find no sleep. In this, however, he was mistaken. He had scarcely stretched himself on the bed when all the weariness and fatigue of the day came upon him, and, as it were with a great wave, swept him into oblivion.

CHAPTER XXVIII.

BY THE FIRELIGHT.

THE moonlight falling upon Gideon as he tramped heavily along the muddy roads that led to Saxton essayed in vain to peep in through the shuttered windows of the bijou residence suitable for a gentleman of fortune and situate off the Fulham Road. The moonlight wouldn't have minded the elaborate contrivances attached to the window shutters, and designed for the surprise of possible burglars, and would cheerily have run the gauntlet of the guillotine arrangements of the front door.

As to the back door, that was secured by bar and bolt, and was made as much as possible like unto the wall. An ordinary bachelor of fortune might have retained for himself the privilege of walking out in sunny days on the small pleasure ground twelve feet by ten, which lay in the rear of the premises. The Spider despised such recreative joys, and the back-yard was accordingly yielded up to the pleasure of sparrows and the growth of weeds, which sprang up through the gravel, threatening to obliterate all trace of it.

What the sparrows found there it was hard to guess. Some people, more particularly in winter weather, put out crumbs for the delectation of the sparrows. That was a thought that had never occurred to the Spider, and if it had he could not conveniently have carried it out, seeing that the door was screwed up. But the sparrows came all the same, twittering about the bare bleak garden ground, and perhaps wondering what it was for—which, indeed, was a thought not absent from the mind of the proprietor, who regarded it as a waste of valuable building ground almost enough of itself to bring a judgment on the house.

The moonlight was not so strong in London

as over the long white road, and the dark cool
fields it illuminated for Gideon's guidance. The
wind was not so fresh in the town as in the
country, and in addition to the regular agglo-
meration of cloud there was the ordinary
contribution of smoke from the mighty kingdom
which for the most part had retired to rest. It
was past midnight here as it was with Gideon
trudging along the road with his hat on the
back of his head, and those mud-stained garments which at any other time would have
caused him poignant distress.

But there were moments when the moonlight, if it could only have stormed the barricade
of the shutter, might have lit up some of the
rooms of the bijou residence, and discovered
what was in them. As for the upper story, it
would not have found much besides dust. The
old gentleman had not gone in largely for
furniture, and what he had possessed himself of
he had for the most part left behind in Carlton
Street, debiting it at cost price to his only son.

Therefore, when, long failing a tenant for the house whose suitability for bachelors of fortune was persistently decried by that class, he came to reside in it himself, he was not met by the necessity for lavish expense claimed by porters, furniture removers, and other harpies, who gather round a dismantled household.

Some people of weak nerves would not have cared to be in those upper rooms at midnight, their footsteps muffled by the thick carpet of dust, and only the moonlight (supposing it could have got in) to light them. Even the knowledge that down on the ground floor was the lively old gentleman, who was sole tenant, would not have altogether removed the feeling of unpleasantness. The rooms smelt so musty, and looked so desolate, and had such strange echoes when their stillness was disturbed by the slightest sound, that even persons of ordinarily strong nerves would have felt a little creeping of the skin and a general desire to get down-stairs, into the company of the old gentleman, though on this particular night he could not reasonably be expected to be found in a good temper.

So, on the whole, it was just as well for the moonlight that it could not get in, and after a while it gave up the quest, passing on down the street, and leaving the bijou residence in dark shadow.

It would be supposed with increased certainty that even if you got in by the front door in a single piece, fortuitously evading the separative tendencies of the old gentleman's masterpiece, you would find everything dark, and everybody gone to bed. Such a conclusion would have demonstrated afresh the danger of hasty generalising. There was no light upstairs, no light in the hall, utter darkness in the little crib at the back of the dining-room originally designed for a lavatory, but now utilised as a place of repose where through summer and winter nights the old gentleman stretched his lively body, slept the sleep of the just, and dreamed alternately that he was being robbed and that he had discovered a gold mine.

But in the front room, where the safe is, and where we had the honour of first making the proprietor's acquaintance, there were both light and company.

The illumination was not much, and was almost as fitful as the moonlight. It came from the rusty grate, and was the generous legacy of light and warmth which Gideon had inadvertently left behind when he emptied the coal-scuttle. That procedure had been very critical, and had long seemed to promise disaster. When Gideon had departed, and after the old gentleman had danced off a little surplus energy and a good deal of slack, he had gone down on his knees and peered through the bars to discover whether there was yet left anything of the fire. It had been, after his manner, exceedingly low when Gideon had performed this ruthless action. Now it seemed out altogether, and the old gentleman gave it up for a bad job.

As he reflected, there are few evil things without some concurrent compensation of good. In the pan which Gideon had noted standing in the grate was a fresh supply of that compound which the Spider proudly denominated ' scouse.' It had been his intent in due time dexterously and delicately to draw the fire together so that sufficient heat might be forthcoming to warm the compound. But since there was no fire how could it be done? and no man, however ravenous his appetite, could be inclined to eat cold scouse. At least if such there were it was not for the Spider to encourage irregularities.

No fire no supper. There it was, any one might see, ready with even ostentatious liberality. There was the cloth spread, the plates handy, the knife and fork displayed, and if by an untoward accident entirely beyond control the fire had gone out, who was to blame, and what measure of reproach might be heaped upon the head of the intending host?

Perhaps if he had promptly taken the slack

off from the top of the fire with a shovel he might have rescued the dim flame from extinction. With the use of a chip of wood this would have been a certain success. But chips were one halfpenny a bundle, and, owing to the progress of education and the consequent drain upon that class of boys engaged in making them, were growing increasingly smaller in bulk.

'The will must go for the deed, to-night,' said the Spider to himself, almost gaily, as he knelt down, and, drawing the scuttle towards him, picked up bit by bit the slack that had become scattered over the floor as the shower descended upon him.

He was not without suspicion that some waste had taken place in respect of particles concealed about his clothing, and even in the scanty locks of hair that struggled out below his skull-cap. But he did his best to grapple with this and other sources of waste, and in the end, with the exception of the overloaded grate, he had pretty well rescued the precious dust.

Now, at the solemn hour when we look in, what time Gideon is standing under the finger-post at the four cross roads and shuddering at its likeness to the gallows, the fire, secretly and maliciously burning in the centre, had taken full possession of the grate, and burned gloriously—probably not quite so gloriously as an hour ago, but still sufficient to cast a warm glow over the hearth, and from time to time, as 'little knubbly bits' fell in from the back, to flame up with a sudden light that filled the remotest corner of the room.

In the fuller light that fell upon the near radius of the fireplace was discernible a shadowy figure sitting in the chair into which the old gentleman had dropped trembling with passion and choking with coal dust, when Gideon stamped out of the room.

It must be the old gentleman himself, though it is passing strange that he should sit up so late, being constitutionally of early habits in this respect, and, more than ever so of late, recognising his ability to save the slack by going early to bed.

In a moment of gay inspiration, the old gentleman had composed a poem on the subject, which at the approach of the hour of separation he was never tired of repeating to Mr. Dumfy, and which never failed to excite the tribute of laughter from that gentleman. It ran thus—

> **Early to bed, lie on your back,**
> **Saves in a year a ton of good slack.**

Since he had the bedclothes, duly paid for and doing nothing, he might as well use them, and they kept him warm without wasteful expenditure, which was not the case in respect of the slack fire howsoe'er tended.

After the surprise at finding the old gentleman up at this time of night comes the still greater marvel that he should sit and see the fire burning in this unprecedented manner, and take no steps to check it. There had been other waste, for it was clear that the solitary dip in the tin candlestick on the table at his elbow had burned down into its socket. And this was only Sunday night, whereas its last flicker was not due till Wednesday at bedtime. It must have been out some time, though there was still palpable in the close atmosphere of the room the odour of the departed wick.

Still the old gentleman sat there, apparently buried in deep thought. Perhaps he was touched with some tender memories of the past, when Gideon played about his knee, a fresh, bright boy, with rosy cheeks, and laughing eyes, and loving caresses.

Why should he have been so hard with him in a moment of dire distress? It would have been nothing to him to have laid his hand on the 3,000*l.* asked for as a temporary loan. He knew the security was safe, and perhaps if the firelight had happened to flash up at the moment it might have brightened up a glow of pride pervading the withered face as he thought how, in his gigantic speculation, his only son had not been unworthy of him. It was well planned and boldly carried out—perhaps a little too boldly, since Gideon's means of handling ready cash had not proved quite equal to the strain upon them. If he had had a father, or even a friend, to come forward just now and help him over the next month or so, the last milestone in the long highway to wealth and honour would have been passed, and the prize would have been in his grasp.

Why should he have been so harsh with the son of his loins, who stood to him even as Benjamin and Joseph towards their father Jacob? Israel had many sons, but whilst his heart was large enough for all, it yearned with unspeakable affection for Joseph and Benjamin.

The old gentleman of late years had returned into full union with that church he had never entirely left. It was just possible that this was the result of fresh obstinacy and contrariness towards his son. Gideon had formally left the church of his fathers, and had joined the Christian community. His father therefore would be more faithful in his attendances at the synagogue, and more punctual in the payment of his dues. He had brought out again the old book, in which was written in Hebrew characters the marvellous story of God's dealings with his race. He had been reading it last night. It was up on the shelf here now, almost within reach of his hand, if he cared to stretch it forth.

He could not fail to remember, if his thoughts were really turned in this direction, how, when taking it down and spreading it open on the table before him to make the most of the ultimate inch of Saturday's candle, he had thought to himself with a sneer that Gideon would scarcely be able to profit by the book even if he were inclined to read it. His wife Rachel had taught the boy the tongue which Israel speaks by whatever dark waters the people may sit. Almost as soon as he could lisp he had learned at her knee the portent of the strange characters spread out before him. But when the mother died the father had not found time to carry on the lessons nor thought it worth while to spend money in having them completed. So Gideon, in the course of time, forgot what little he had learned, and did not seem to feel the loss.

But the old gentleman could read Hebrew as well as he could read English, and sometimes in his solitude read out aloud, in a croning voice, passages from the old book. On the night before he had, by chance, been reading the story of Joseph. He had begun at the beginning, when the news is brought to the father by the wicked brethren.

' And Jacob rent his clothes and put sackcloth upon his loins, and mourned for his son many days. And all his sons and all his daughters rose up to comfort him; but he refused to be comforted, and he said, " For I will go down to the grave unto my son mourning." Thus his father wept for him.'

And thus the old man, sitting in his lonely room—calculating even as he read how long the candle would last—felt unwonted moisture in his eyes and began to think with strange tenderness of the son whom he had driven from his door, when a little while ago he had called to see him.

The old man had read on rapidly, skipping passages, till he came to the verses where the father sits mourning over Joseph, or clings with miserly affection to Benjamin when he is claimed by the strange ruler in Egypt.

To the world this is the story of Joseph and his Brethren. To the Spider it was the story of Israel and his Sons. He had read it often before, but never as now. It was all new to him, with fresh lights and awakened interest.

He had read aloud with a broken voice how ' they told him saying Joseph is yet alive, and he is governor over all the land of Egypt; and Jacob's heart fainted, for he believed them not. And they told him all the words of Joseph which he had said unto them, and when he saw the waggons which Joseph had sent to carry him to Egypt Israel said, " It is enough ! Joseph, my son, is yet alive, I will go and see him before I die." '

If Gideon could have come in at that moment a reconciliation might have been effected. But this was not to be, and the opportunity was gone when the candle flickered out and the Spider awoke to the fact that he had left several things undone which he must now accomplish in the dark, because he had permitted this unaccustomed weakness to over-come him.

All this had happened last night. And now everything was too late. Gideon had insulted him, even assaulted him. But who was the earlier aggressor? His son had come to him in trouble, if not in contrition. And what had he done? He had befooled him, had even spat upon him ; and was Gideon a dog that he could tamely submit? He might have refused his prayer without contumely; but why refuse it at all?

There in the shade which the flickering firelight fitfully illumined stood the safe, in which there was something more than the 3,000*l*. Gideon had asked for, the bulk in gold as he had maliciously shown his son, and besides this, in a snug recess at the back, was a pile of bank notes as thick as the old Hebrew Bible.

Yet it was hard to forgive and impossible to forget. Gideon had wounded him sorely. It was as if the treachery had been slowly and deliberately worked out, and then flashed upon him at a time when he was both powerless and unsuspecting. From the day he took the lad into the office till the hour at which he himself had walked out having relinquished the business to Gideon, the youth's career had been full of promise. He was assiduous in business, bringing to it a fresher mind and bolder and more energetic nature, than those his father had worn out at the task of money-getting. He had promised to extend to an illimitable measure the fame of the house the Spider had founded.

There were already great houses in Israel whose names were familiar words on all continents, and whose nod shook the Bourse. Why should not the little dingy house in Carlton Street blossom into a second Rothschild's? They, and others only second to them, did not begin from greater opportunities.

It might have been so, and he fondly hoped, as he watched the promising growth of his lad, that it would be so. Believing this he had deliberately stepped aside out of the way dear to his soul, and the only pathway of his life, in order that no old-fashioned notions of his own might stand in the way of Gideon's brilliant and successful advance.

For a year all had gone well, and the picture that illumined his mind and uplifted his hopes grew clearer in outline, and stronger in colour. Then the Evil One had come and tempted Gideon, drawing him aside from his father's work and possessing him with a fatal hankering for the flesh-pots of Egypt.

The Spider did not, though this was not to be gathered from his conversation, object to the great land speculation. Towards this his soul secretly kindled, and, if that had been all, all would have been well. He would have grumbled, and might even have charged a stiff percentage on the loan. But he would certainly not have sent his son empty away.

What he could not stand, and what made him grind his teeth with impotent rage, was the notion that a son of his should go crawling and fawning at the door of the Gentile of rank and fashion, and beg to be let in on whatsoever terms.

This grievously smote the prejudices and animosities of the old man's nature. In the first place, it seemed to imply that Gideon was ashamed of his origin, his race, and his father.

The new departure had been immediately preceded by Gideon's changing his name, an act which above all seared the soul of the old Israelite. Byond these incidental circumstances, he honestly despised birth and rank, which he was chiefly accustomed to see suppliant for money loans in Carlton Street.

If it came to a question of birth, what were these Gentiles compared with him ? His house might be humble enough now, but its annals were traced with more or less clearness back to the epoch of the Captivity. She who had become the mother of his race had been among the virgins of Babylon who wept for their far-off home and the dimmed splendours of the Temple. To have his son scraping acquaintance with haughty purse-proud English people who had not even come over with the Conqueror, and could not, therefore, boast that they had persecuted the Jews when Isaac lived at York, was more than he could bear, and perhaps, if we could have caught the expression of his face as the firelight fitfully played upon it, we might have seen the old look that accompanied the snarl.

Finally all this cost money. If Gideon had been content to live in Carlton Street and creep along in the old style till he was in a position to pay off his mortgages, it would not have been so bad if thereafter he blossomed forth into butterfly form. But on each alternate Sunday Mr. Dumfy, as he ate his scouse and drank his pint of four-half, regaled the ear of his host with stories, scarcely exaggerated, of Gideon's lavish expenditure.

It was torture to the old man to hear this; and yet as children, sitting by the firelight or clinging to each other in the dark, like to hear ghost stories that chill their very marrow, so he listened to every detail of Gideon's iniquity. He knew all about the public-house taps flowing with ale or porter. He heard more than was true of great fees paid to Napper's father, and be sure he was informed of Napper's designs on a marriageable man who was actually owner of Castle Fleyce, and prospective heir to the property of a millionaire father, who lived in dirt and obscurity somewhere in London.

Mr. Dumfy, who was a great artist, well knew the impressive effect of this last bit of colour. He therefore reserved it for particular occasions, and the nett result was that the Spider had constantly in his mind the picture of Gideon waiting for his death, gloating over the prospects of coming into his large possession, and luring on a designing girl with promises of illimitable wealth when the old man was out of the way.

This was running into an evil groove of thought, away from the moment when the old hard, steel-glittering eyes might have had their keenness dimmed at the thought of Israel's yearnings after his long-lost son, and his joyful haste to go forth to meet him. It was sad, and black, and hopeless, and the sadder for sitting in the bare and squalid room, from which even the tallow candle in the tin stick had fled.

When we come to think of it, there is small wonder that the old man should sit thus in fixed and mournful meditation. It was his own fault, but which of us can help his idiosyncrasies? As the twig is bent so will the tree be inclined. The Spider had been bent in his particular way by the previous training of father, grandfather, and great-grandfather. Far back through musty corridors of time might be seen young and old steadily and feverishly working at money-getting.

One not so far back in the corridor (it was the Spider's father) went about his task with a dirty sack over his shoulder, two hats rim to rim in his hand, and three more on his head. He was not a dignified, but rather a dirty-looking person. Yet he found what he wanted, and when the sack fell off his bowed shoulders, and the hats were put down for the last time, and when he turned his face to the wall, the Spider had been able to watch his last moments with the filial affection born of the certainty that he had put out at usury in safe hands a sum that could not be a penny less than 3,000*l*.

This had come to the Spider, and see what he had made? Should this aggregate of the hard, and more or less strictly honest, work of two generations, go to a fellow like Gideon, who would give 3*l*. for a man's vote, and smilingly bid the borough come and drink at his expense?

It was, then, small wonder that the old gentleman should sit in fixed and mournful meditation. The firelight, rising into flame as the little bits of slack on the black rim that surrounded the crater crumbled and fell in, flashed a momentary light into the corners of the room. Anon it left all in shade, save what was rescued by the steady glow that fell on the hearth and warmed the old gentleman's slippered feet.

When the flashes came they fell upon the rusty velvet skull-cap and the old grey coat that seemed never the worse for wear, perhaps

because its earliest known condition was hopeless.   The room was absolutely still.   Not even
a mouse scampering across the boards disturbed the silence.   If the old gentleman had
fallen asleep in his chair, and was given to
breathing heavily, the sound must have been
heard in any part of the room.

Perhaps when the next flash came with
a slight rustling noise of the falling slack he
would wake with a start, gather his old cloak
around him, and creep steadily to bed, anguished
by the thought that sleep had unaccountably
overcome him and had led to this wicked waste
of fire and candle.

But he was evidently not asleep, for, as the
last flash of firelight showed, his eyes were wide
open and fixed with eager glance upon that
part of the room in which, for the most part in
shadow, the safe stood.

The expression on his face, though curiously
fixed, made it nonsense to suppose he was asleep.
If he were asleep he must be dreaming, or even

he may have the nightmare. Who knows but what, tempted by the presence of the food in the pan, he may have taken some, with consequences that any outsider might have anticipated? It was cooked, it is true, being the remnants of his midday meal prepared on an exceptionally bountiful scale in anticipation of an evening festival. But cold meat and potatoes, taken late at night by a gentleman well advanced in years, and unaccustomed to eat anything after a frugal five-o'clock tea, could not fail to have its certain effect.

Let us lift up the lid of the pan and peer in. No; there is the precious compound evidently untouched, a great deal of potato, a very little meat, and a large bone, which has a juicy, nutritive appearance wholly inconsistent with fact. If we had been here at one o'clock in the day we would have seen this same bone in the old gentleman's dirty fingers, and when the Spider once got a bone between his teeth he was not accustomed to leave much meat for

those who came after. It was a mere matter
of form to return it to the mess. But it added
a completeness to the compound, and, when
splashed about with potato, gave an air of tooth-
some liberality to the meal which was otherwise
lacking.

Without troubling to lift the lid of the pan
we might have seen by a glance at the table
that the old gentleman had fallen asleep supper-
less. There was the dingy cloth obscuring one
end of the still dingier table, even as Gideon
had discovered it when he entered. There
was the plate as clean as crockery ever was in
the bijou residence. There was the bread uncut,
and difficult to cut now, for the knife was gone,
only the three-pronged steel fork lying by the
side of the plate.

It was a curious knife, valuable in its way,
and the Spider, before sinking into contemplation, very likely put it in a safe place. It had
been in its time a dagger, and knew the grasp of
an eminently respectable member of the nobility

of Genoa. The Spider's information did not particularly run in the direction of bric-à-brac. But seeing the knife lying exposed for sale in a cellar window in the Commercial Road, he had gone in and bought it.

When his solitary specimen of English table cutlery had broken off at the hilt, he had got on tolerably well for some time by the expedient of sticking a cork on the broken stem of the handle. But this gave him very little hold. Then he bethought him of his old bargain in the Commercial Road, cleaned it up, and used it at his daily meal. It didn't cut very well, but had a good sharp dagger point, and gave a splendid grip at the handle.

In his genial way he used to joke with Mr. Dumfy about the splendour of his state, eating his supper with a knife like that.

'There's many a man at the West End would give you the finest supper in the world if you would let him eat his with that knife, Mr. Dumfy,' he had been used to say when he saw

his guest critically eyeing the measure of four-
half or somewhat ostentatiously probing about
in the sea of potato for a morsel of meat.

'It's very 'andsome, sir, and I dessay worth
a lot, but when it comes to eating your supper,
especially if the meat's a little stringy, I would
as lief have one of them black-handled things
as me and the missus eats our meals with in our
'umble way.'

Evidently the Spider had not eaten his
supper, and since it was not that it must have
been something else that had disagreed with
him. At times, when the light fell upon his
face, it seemed that he was glowering with
unfeigned hate and horrible fury. But in the
fuller light, or perhaps in the varying movement
of his mind, this phase passed away, and was
supplanted by another expression.

There was upon his face now a look of
fierce and almost malignant joy, which, taken
in conjunction with his steady gaze, suggested
that he was staring at something that pleased

him beyond measure. The thin lips were parted and distorted with a smile not pleasing to look upon. Yet, catching again the look of strange and almost fiendish joy which the fire-light lit up in his countenance, it was evident he was not thinking kindly of any person.

It did not seem that there was anything in his interview with his son to account for his present frame of mind. There was, of course, the pitfall into which he had led Gideon, with the added depth dug by his getting out of him the receipt stamp which he was careful to spoil. But this was a slight cause to bring about this remarkable effect.

Following the unvarying gaze of the old gentleman, it was clear that his eyes were fixed upon the safe, though he never blinked nor moved his head when sometimes the light, flashing forth from the grate, played over the safe, and momentarily dying out left it in the gloom. When once the attention was drawn towards the expression on the face of the old gentleman, you would discover your mistake in supposing it had changed with the dancing firelight. The aspect of the room varied with the shifting light, but the old gentleman's face was always the same, ever staring with steady regard towards the safe, and always with this same look of malignant joy.

Were there things in the room that only he could see? Were there travelling ghosts about, and were they playing some pranks that tickled the old gentleman's midriff, and brought about this look of hideous mirth? It could hardly have been an ordinary farce, or anything simply funny, which the old gentleman saw. If he were of that curious kind of humanity which finds food for mirth in horrible tragedy, that would supply, or rather suggest, an explanation of his attitude and of the expression on his sallow and dirt-stained face.

But to human eyesight there was nothing in the room between him and the safe. As for the safe, it seemed pretty much as it had been left when Gideon quitted the house. The door was partly open, and the key was in it.

Perhaps what the old gentleman was staring at in this horribly fixed manner was the odd condition of the key. Either the flickering light distorted it, or, as a matter of fact, it was bent downwards in the lock as if some heavy body hanging on to the bow had, after a desperate struggle, been dragged away.

This might have been, and possibly was, a delusion created by the firelight, which has long been known to give birth to a series of eccentric fancies. There was, however, scarcely any room for delusion as to some other things which come to be noticed when we are attracted by the discovery of the old gentleman, whose lively disposition made it on ordinary occasions impossible for him to sit still a moment, ever remaining in a fixed position.

The firelight flickered about the figure in the armchair, running up and down the right arm as it rested on the elbow, and passed upward to

the extended hand.   There it showed a strange
thing.   The hand was firmly clenched, and
between the fingers was held the lapel of a coat.
This, it seemed, had been snatched by a sudden
wrench from the garment, and, quite clearly
when the firelight flamed forth, were visible
the jagged ends where the rent had been made,
whilst the bony fingers of the small dirty hand
held the cloth as in a vice.

Something else the firelight played upon—
something of metal, which might have remained
hidden but for occasional flashes on steel facets.
This was the handle of the Genoese knife which
had been lying on the table when Gideon
entered, and which he had for a moment taken
up and balanced in his hand, absently looking
upon it as if he were thinking of something else
than the metal on the haft.

The surmise ventured upon just now that
the old gentleman had put the knife away in a
safe place turned out to be quite correct.   He
had put it in his breast, doubtless intending to

lay it aside in some cupboard when, by-and-bye, he should get up and go to bed.

Another strange effect of the firelight, and not the least, was that it seemed he had thrust the knife straight in up to the hilt. Else how could it stand out at right angles with the old brown coat, and so give fuller opportunity for the firelight to play about the bright places on the haft, where daily use had rubbed off the dust of ages ?

CHAPTER XXIX.

AN UNEXPECTED MEETING.

THE morning broke bright and fair, after the manner of mornings without reference to what may have taken place on the previous night. That is not their affair. Let the night keep its own secrets and if need be bury its own dead. The morning will have nothing to do with them. All sorts of evil things may have taken place during the dark hours of the night. The more reason that the morning should present itself with an innocent smile and a freshness wholly incompatible with guilt.

After its night-long struggle with the clouds the wind had finally triumphed, had blown them all away inland or out to sea, anywhere away from Saxton. It was cold, of course.

March does not pretend to be anything else. Still there was a breath of spring in the air, and Knut gambolled about in ecstatic delight. No one to look at that dog would suppose for a moment that he had been out the greater part of the night, and had nearly nipped by the calf of the leg the proprietor of the neighbouring château.

Nor for the matter of that would any one have suspected Mr. Tandy of nocturnal rambling. He had come down to his breakfast at the usual hour, had sat opposite Napper and the coffee urn, in his accustomed way, and had thereafter appeared at his office at the ordinary time.

Breakfast was not the lively meal it used to be. There was nothing like open rupture or even constant coldness between Napper and her father. To casual observers she was just the same, careful for all his comforts, interested in all his topics, and as pleasant a companion as man might desire to see at his breakfast table.

Only the guilty breast of Mr. Tandy told him that there was a change, and that Napper was angry with him, which was not true. Napper was sorry, not angry, and there are times when we would rather those we love were angry with us than that they should sorrow about us.

It was not for Napper to judge her father. That she honestly felt, and daily fought against tendencies in the contrary direction. But he was not quite the same to her that he had been when she trained his elephantine movements in the mazes of the giddy waltz, or taught him to uplift his hippopotamic voice in ordered melody. Napper resisted all temptations to judge. But she could not help feeling, and she felt that it was wrong for her father not only to associate himself with people who were buying votes for money or beer, but, worse still, to take an active part in the enterprise.

All the misery and degradation wrought in the borough had within the last few days been brought to a head by an incident which had greatly heightened the excitement and rancour of the contested election. Long Bill had come to an untimely end. It had been proudly thought down at the beach that Long Bill was proof against any accumulation of spirituous liquor.

'You might put him in a spirit wat for twenty-four hour, and he'd come out wiping his lips, and asking if ye 'ad a quart of small beer 'andy.'

Thus, with an inflection of honest emotion in his voice, spoke Round Tommy, the dead hero's companion in many a sturdy bout.

But Long Bill had succumbed, and after a manner that will make his fate ever memorable. What with constantly moving round the flag-staff at the Blue Lion, and describing circles that invariably led him to the tap-room, Long Bill had become a little disordered in mind and body. He began to talk wildly, and on one occasion was observed carefully wheeling a barrow of old rope up and down High Street

The next discovery was that of Long Bill pendant in the stables attached to the Blue Lion. He had been cut down with remarkable promptitude, but he had taken rope enough, and had hanged himself.

All this was bad, but there was worse to follow. An inquest was held, and by some chance, unforeseen at the time, it was packed with adherents of the Conservative cause. These good citizens, remembering Long Bill's strenuous exertions on the other side, were not inclined to extend to him the privilege of insanity. It was in vain that Mr. Tandy, who had taken up the cause with great zest, brought forward witnesses who testified to the strangeness of deceased's conduct during the past week. The jury were a little shaken at the testimony given on oath of Long Bill's having been seen wheeling about a heavily laden barrow. It was felt that if he really had come to do a hard day's work it could scarcely be whilst in his ordinary condition of mind. But political animosity prevailed. Verdict of *felo de se* was brought in, and, in fulfilment of the barbarous law which then existed, Long Bill was buried at midnight in unconsecrated ground.

Probably it was no great matter to Long Bill where he was laid to rest after his battle of life was done, and his long and faithful watch for the ship that never came in had reached a close. To Gideon it was, at first sight, the loss of various money payments and much miscellaneous drink. His majority would be one the less since Long Bill could not make his cross on the ballot paper and exercise the right of the free-born Englishman, who is also a householder and has paid his rates. It was as if he had, regardless of expense, freighted a ship, and just when she was approaching the harbour, and his reward seemed forthcoming, she had gone down carrying everything with her.

Long Bill had gone down, and regarded as an investment he was a dead loss. But Gideon

was keen enough to seize his opportunity in the
harsh verdict of the coroner's jury, and had
made the most of it.   He had appeared on the
scene at midnight when the funeral took place,
had, in fact, dressed in deep mourning, and,
with a long band of crape drooping from his
hat, headed the procession which followed Long
Bill to the grave.

'This is worth fifty votes to us,' he had
said to Mr. Tandy as the two stood aside watching the heaving, angry crowd, who at one time
threatened to make a dash at the coffin, dig a
grave in consecrated ground, and compel the
rector to recite over the six feet two of Long
Bill's stiff humanity that service which was
his right, though he had not cared to claim
much spiritual comfort from the Church whilst
alive.

Gideon did not want to create a riot.   Everything that was desirable to be done had been
accomplished, and by his personal interposition
the sorry business ended amid howls and hoots

for the jury, groans for poor, innocent Mr. Montgomery, and cheers for the Liberal candidate. Gideon's conduct on this occasion was in due time recorded in the press, and was calculated to secure for him the approval of all right-thinking people.

Long Bill was no favourite of Napper's. If a week ago she had been asked to declare her opinion of him, it would have gone hard against him as an idle, good-for-nothing fellow, who hung about the beach with his hands in his pockets by day, drank more than was good for him at night, and had pushed to their farthest limits the opportunities opened to him by election times. But now she saw in him a victim of the system which permitted such things to go on, and tried hard, but not altogether successfully, to keep back the thought that her father was in some respects responsible for Long Bill's melancholy end and his shameful burial.

Therefore, Napper had not cared to extend the breakfast hour, and when it was decently over, and her father had shut himself up in his office, Knut was observed making a dash up the street and round the block of houses which the neighbours knew preluded an excursion on the part of his mistress.

Napper used to find a familiar walk up the hill, past the ruined Castle, and beyond the woods where the wild flowers came earliest, and where the birds first woke with the glad surprise that spring had come again. Now she had come to hate that way, and carefully avoided it. She had once taken great pride in the alterations of the Castle, feeling a just satisfaction at the knowledge that owing to her they had been carried out without injury to the grave beauty of the structure. Except that there was something new beside the ruin the Castle was as beautiful now as when Gideon's eyes had first lighted up with the thought that he would connect himself and his name with the old place.

Napper could not bear the man or his

place, and when she walked she bore away to the bleaker side, where the Downs looked over the marshes, on to the far-off waste that was the sea.

Knut was not at all particular, and would go anywhere so that he had Napper to revolve round as the moving object of his desperate rushing to and fro.

Napper got rid of her troubles when out of Saxton, and walked along with her head well up, a glow on her cheeks and a great desire in her heart to laugh and be merry. Just now she was cut off from opportunities for cheerful conversation. All her idols had been detected with feet of clay, at which she could no longer sit. In this sad case she found much comfort in the company of Knut, and with him out in the fields where the grass was turning to a brighter green, and where the hedges and trees were beginning to wake up to the new life that would last a whole summer, Napper was herself again.

'Why don't *you* have a vote, Knut?' she said. 'I do believe if you had you would give it honestly, which would be quite a strange thing in these parts. One thing I am certain of, you would not sell it for beer, though what might happen if you were offered a bone for your vote and interest, I daren't guess. Water for you, pure water for you, otherwise mixed with a little milk. Then you don't care for money. You don't fawn on people for what you can get out of them. You have a wonderful eye for what Mr. Carlyle calls the Good and the True, which by the way accounts for your strong affection for me. Moreover, you have a wholesome tendency to take a bite out of whatever for the moment represents the False and the Base. You cannot do much, my poor old dog, but every little helps. I'm sure your notion is that if you take a bite here and a bite there out of the legs of mean people you will in time reduce the average going about. I dismiss that unworthy suspicion about the bone, and declare that if you had a vote you would give it to the best man regardless of bribes. Perhaps there might be some difficulty in informing you on political questions. On Foreign Policy I'm sure you would go about blindly. But it does not seem to me that that would make much difference as compared with those who have the franchise now. I wonder what Long Bill thought of the Concordat, or what are Round Tommy's views on the Treaty of Berlin? I am sure I don't know anything about them myself. I am not quite certain that the Concordat, whatever it may be, has anything to do with us just now. But that it is just the position of more than one half of the men who will say next week whether Mr. Fleyce is to be our member, or whether Mr. Montgomery shall continue to represent us. I declare I would rather Mr. Montgomery kept his place. He at least has been brought up as a gentleman, and though he is very stupid, and his chief notion of going to Parliament is to make himself comfortable, his position assures him against the necessity of pretending so much and telling quite so many lies as Mr. Fleyce seems to have to do. Which would you vote for, Knut, supposing you were on the register?'

Knut had listened to the earlier portion of these remarks with lively interest. He had barked his approval and had found other means of expression of the perfect concord of feeling on these points as on others. But instead of waiting to answer this crucial question he had pricked up his ears and bounded off at the top of his speed, and was presently returning the salutation of Mr. Jack Bailey, whom he had discovered walking down the road.

Now this, if every one had known it, was a most peculiar concurrence of place and time for Jack to find himself in. A very short time ago, in fact when Knut was making that desperate dash which preluded the appearance of Miss Tandy, Jack had, by the merest chance, been standing within the portico of the Town-hall, apparently absorbed in profound study of a list of the polling places proclaimed under the hand of the Mayor of Saxton.

This could not have conveyed to Jack's mind much information that was novel. The document had been out for some days, and a copy of it had, in fact, appeared in the 'Saxton Beacon,' and Jack had written a brief editorial calling attention to the localities, and urging Liberal electors to make preparations for an early appearance. Moreover, Jack had been there long enough to enable him, if he had acutely felt the desire, to learn off the list by heart.

Still, he stood at gaze, in no way like Joshua's sun at Ajalon except in respect of absolute fixity. It was so far fortunate that Jack should have happened to be on the spot just now that he chanced to see Knut dash out and recognised the signal of Miss Tandy's approach. Being on friendly terms with the young lady, it might have been supposed that when, presently, she herself appeared and began to walk down the street in the direction of the Town-hall, Jack would have advanced to meet her, and to have offered some remarks upon the weather.

But Jack had not forgotten the result of an earlier endeavour of that kind. He was too high-spirited to place himself in a position where repulse might be repeated. He stood till he saw Napper well advanced along the street, which had its only exit on the high road that presently led over the Downs, and then, taking a narrow lane that bisected the town, led up to the church, and so away into the country, he disappeared.

Napper, if she had been aware of this strategic retreat—and, strange as it may appear to some young ladies, she really knew nothing —would have regarded it with distinct approval. Here was Jack, whilst engaged in the pursuit of his ordinary avocations, suddenly and unexpectedly approached by a young lady whom he madly loved, but who wholly disregarded his passion. Was it for him to throw himself in her way and plaintively endeavour to induce her to reconsider her position? Miss Tandy, if the case had been put to her, would have emphatically answered in the negative. She liked the spirit of the youth who declared that

> If she be not fair to me,
> What care I how fair she be?

That was the proper and manly way to look at circumstances in which Jack unhappily found himself, and when, being thus inexplicably caught, he turned and walked rapidly away, careful to avoid an encounter that might have brought him humiliation, he did a very proper thing.

CHAPTER XXX.

EDITORIAL CARES.

ALL this made it the more remarkable that at this very moment, here in this remote place, Jack should have been discovered right in the pathway of Destruction, which advanced towards him with a pretty smile and kindly look of recognition. His strategic retreat had, by strange mischance, brought him right within the enemy's lines.

Napper happened to be in the mood to welcome Jack. She had not seen him lately, which, though it was not pleasant to say so, was a point in his favour. Besides, it was a different thing meeting him in this chance way, without the preliminary of request, formally made, that he might accompany her and Knut on an excursion. Then, having to make the choice, and her new sorrow being fresh upon her, making her a little petulant, she had said, ' No! ' a monosyllable that smote Jack with a sudden pain that could not have been excelled by a lash falling across his shoulders.

Now, he and she, in the oddest way in the world, met in a country lane on a bright spring morning, at a moment when Napper's spirits had been raised by fresh air and exercise, and when she had actually been driven for lack of other companion to talk to Knut.

Jack, who looked unaccountably guilty at first, was quick to see this, and soon recovered his equanimity.

' Why, Mr. Bailey, who would have thought of meeting you here ! ' she cried, holding out to Jack a little gloved hand which he had great difficulty in returning to its owner.

Possession he felt was nine points of the law ; but on reflection he decided to be honest. There were penalties in the present case besides those which the law assigns to highway robbery. If he began by holding Miss Napper's hand longer than the usages of society warranted, she would take fright at the outset, and there would be a sudden end to the encounter which had so fortunately opened.

'I dare say you were not thinking of me, Miss Tandy,' said Jack, a little ruefully. 'That would be too much to hope for. The fact is, Monday's an idle day with me, or comparatively idle. I'm always working; but you see in our profession one need not always have his tools in his hand.'

'Now that's very convenient. Yours must be an excellent profession for a man who does not love work. If we found old Tom Nollekins, who does up our garden, standing with his hands in his pockets, intently gazing on a sun-flower, we should think he was idling, and would be quite sure of it if we found him lying on his back on a hot summer day gazing up at the sky. But, of course, you might do either of these things without imputation on your industry. Perhaps now I am interrupting the incubation—is that the word?—of a leading article. I dare say at the moment I saw you you were just tripping up Lord Beaconsfield, and my unfortunate choice of this road for a walk may have led to a further postponement of his fall. So Knut and I will go our way and leave you to struggle with Apollyon.'

'Indeed, I was not doing anything of the kind. What I mean is that when people work as tremendously with their brain as I do, they must take a little exercise. Accordingly on a Monday I make it a point of going out for a stroll.'

'You must have been a good long walk this morning—as far as Felton at least, and that way round out of the town is a good twelve miles.'

'Quite, I should think,' said Jack, blushing with the consciousness of recent racing up the narrow and steep backway out of the town, the scramble over the road, the run across the field, and the fortuitous deliverance out upon the highway which led to Felton, and thence by the Gatesand Road which approached the town by the other side. 'But I'm not a bit tired. In fact, when I was at college I was a don at walking or running, and thought nothing of my twenty-five miles a day. It's rather fortunate for me I met you. I wanted to ask your opinion about the "Beacon" generally, and if you don't mind I'll stroll along with you a bit.'

Napper, as it happened, did not greatly mind. Moreover, if she had done so, Jack had overcome possible hesitancy by adroitly turning round some moments earlier, and walking back along the path where he had been descried by Knut. Napper had already for a moment or two been walking by his side, and knew no reason in the world why she should object to the proposed company.

'How do you like the "Beacon," Miss Tandy?'

'Well, to tell the truth, I only read a

portion of it, and that just now is very limited. I never look at anything about the election, of which I am sick and ashamed. This gives me more time to study other parts of the paper. I see you have found a poet who seems to possess in a large measure the attribute of sorrow which is the common property of the poetic soul. I suppose he's a local genius?'

Jack Bailey had recently acquired, or perhaps regained, a habit of blushing. He felt an attack of his weakness now, having a painful consciousness of a little verseling that had appeared in the last number. It was called 'Wan and One,' and thus its tuneful numbers coursed :—

> On Avon's banks the wan wild goose
>   Maketh its weird woe-cry:
> But never more on Avon's bank
>   Walk my One Love and I.
>   *   *   *   *
> On Avon's banks there flits a ghost
>   For ever and for aye!
> The wan Wraith of the welded hearts
>   Of my One Love and I.

' Yes, most country papers have their poets'
corner,' he said, evading the direct question.
' What do you think of our contributor's " Wan
and One "?'

' I thought it quite too-too,' said Napper,
laughing. ' What does the poet mean by the
asterisks in the middle? Is that some other
verses you left out because they were so bad?'

' No; it was printed just as it came in. I
fancy that is a device meant to excite the
imagination. Between the first verse and the
last you must picture the history of a broken
heart. There is the happy meeting by the
river, then comes, perhaps, a false friend, a
misunderstanding, possibly death. The two
are parted. The river rolls on darkly, everything around is the same, but those two
stand apart for ever more. You will find
the same idea in Jean Ingelow's " Divided,"
though there the idea is worked out in a more
elaborate, and perhaps some people may think
a more commonplace, fashion. In this little

poem I fancy the idea of the poet is to gain his effect by bold abrupt touches. In poetry there is the Turneresque style, just as in painting. If you get a little thing of Meissonnier's there it is complete, with every detail worked out. You may go over it with a microscope, and find nothing lacking. With Turner it is, of course, different. A splash here and a blur there, and you have his picture. Turner, if I may say so, makes a lavish use of asterisks in his pictures.'

'Your poet finds a sympathetic editor,' said Napper, looking at him curiously and beginning to suspect the truth.

'If that is the case, I assure you it is an exception. As a rule I am held in detestation, as presumptuously exacting. I believe I have made more enemies since I took to editing this wretched little sheet than ever I did in the preceding twenty-three years of a well-spent life. I have often heard it said that every one thinks he or she can write for a newspaper: now I know it. Next to the amazing unsuitability of what they send in is the illimitable acrimony with which they pursue you for not printing their stuff.'

'Then I suppose this poet has some hold upon you, and you are obliged to print what he sends you?' Napper asked innocently, but with more malice in her heart than usually found lodgment there.

'You are a little hard upon our poet, Miss Tandy. You should see the labours of some of his competitors. But it is the prose contributions that give most trouble. It is really astounding to see what a fool an ordinarily able and shrewd man makes of himself when he becomes possessed with the idea that he can write for the newspapers. I dare say many could if they would be content to write in their ordinary style, as they might to an habitual correspondent. But the notion of writing for print inflates them in a most ridiculous manner. There's our friend Fleyce,

for example, a man I don't like, I freely
confess, but who is not without common sense
and shrewdness. Yet he thinks he can write
as well as any of those " newspaper fellows," and
is, I know, secretly convinced that if he were
not too busy with other affairs he would soon
show Saxton what good writing is. In fact, he
has found time partly to make the demonstra-
tion, and that is one of the things I wanted
to ask you about. You know he went to the
funeral of Long Bill, which was well enough in
its way as a smart electioneering dodge. But
when he got home he was, or thought he was,
so deeply impressed by the scene that he felt
no other hand but his could tune it. We
had a fellow there to do it, but on Sunday
morning before church time I got a letter from
Fleyce inclosing me a lot of manuscript. He'd
been sitting up all night, and sent me an
account of the affair which, as he says, is likely
to make a little stir. I'll just read you a bit of
it, if you don't mind.'

'I certainly don't care to hear anything of or from Mr. Fleyce.'

'Don't you really!' cried Jack, with a sudden illumination of his face, over which had gathered a dark gloom as he thought of Gideon's prose production. 'Then it's all over—I mean, there was nothing in it?'

'Nothing in what, Mr. Bailey?' Napper asked, looking him full in the face, with an expression of simple inquiry, which Jack, with a great throb of his heart, knew was genuine.

He, of course, like Mr. Dumfy and his friends, had noted the intimacy of the proprietor of Castle Fleyce with Miss Tandy. He was quite right in supposing that Gideon meant business, and though he felt that no woman worthy of his (Jack Bailey's) deepest affections could love a man like Fleyce, yet he knew there were other considerations which sometimes brought about marriages.

Of late, as he also knew, this intimacy had ceased. Napper went no more to the Castle, nor any more brought anguish to the souls of the six young men of Saxton and its neighbourhood by being discovered taking country walks with Gideon, or being driven by him in his phaeton. Of course that might have been a mere episode in the regular advance towards matrimony. It may have been a line of asterisks leading up to other conclusions than that pictured in the poem.

But when Napper looked like this and spoke in this natural voice Jack knew that there had been a mistake somewhere, and felt that his way had suddenly grown clearer.

' Oh, nothing, you know, quite nothing. I was thinking at the time of your supposed interest in Mr. Fleyce's candidature. You used to go about with him and show him the places and introduce him to the electors.'

' I didn't quite know that was my mission,' said Napper, walking a little more resolutely and with a shade of annoyance on her face. ' I was a foolish girl, and thought people meant what they said, and were what they represented themselves to be. I thought Mr. Fleyce was coming here to make people freer from prejudice and from other bonds, and perhaps I showed an undesirably warm interest in his projects. But that only proves how ignorant I am, and what comes of people meddling in affairs of which they know nothing. We need not discuss the matter, Mr. Bailey, only I am sorry to know that people in the town should have thought I went too far.'

'Too far!' cried the unhappy Jack, who felt he was always putting his foot in it. 'On the contrary, not far enough—I mean you did exactly what was right. But I was going to read you this picturesque article of Mr. Fleyce's, which has nothing to do with the election, at least not directly. You will remember his address to the electors. That was a pretty fine specimen of prose. This is in another manner, and, I think, excels it. I won't impose the introduction on you, but here we are at the grave which we have reached "with the pro-cession whose sinuous length, snakelike, has extended the full length of the main street of our ancient borough." It is headed "The Scene at the Grave," and I think you will like it.'

Jack read on in an impressive voice the following beautiful passage :—

' "The news had spread like wildfire, and the air was thick with the breath of hundreds. The stillness of the night was broken by the fall of some sere leaf, the rustle of some sparrow in the hedge, the creak of the heavy gate as it groans lazily swinging on its hinges, the mur-mur of the ever-growing crowd, and the sharp click, click of the navvy's spade as it snatches the soil from its bosom. The sight is weird and ghastly. Click, click, under the dim hazy light of the lanthorn. Click, click, as the clammy, sticky clod gives way. Click, click, as the sob of a broken heart falls choking on the weed.

' " The dewy darkness of the night shows up against the flashing helmets of the police arranged in simple cordon round the grave. The road is just like watered silk, with here a streak of gritty flint, and there a brimming pool ; and as the purple bearded clouds roll away from the light of the heaven, the moon's lambent beams play lonely on the watery way. The stream was moaning incessantly. Around the fringe of stunted trees is breathing a dark and sickening scent. Everything is orderly and quiet. The hearse is resting in the portico until the men have done. Midnight is nearing, and the grave is barely half its rightful depth.

' " Impatiently the heaving crowd of spectators swings heavily forward. The coffin is borne on the shoulders of the men, and the body is lowered on the web. Never a service was read, and never an anthem was sung. The voice of indignation is rising in the breast, the crowd sweeps on as if to wrest from its chill embrace the body of the one they loved in life, and from whom in death the verdict of a jury will not part them. The hon. gentleman who stands for this ancient borough in the Liberal interest now spoke a few timely words, urging the surging multitude to let all the guilt of the night rest with the other side, and not smirch the principles of civil and religious liberty with riot, however richly deserved. The crowd swayed respondent to the tongue of true eloquence.

' " The heart is pent, and the hand is held back, and a hush falls on the mass of life among the dead bathed in the mournful glory of the waning lamp. The sod thuds heavily on the coffin lid, a ridging bank of clay rears low to mark the spot. They linger for a time as if a spell had bound them to the grave, or gather into groups, or guiltily steal away, brushing their hands in the hedge, brimful of tears." '

CHAPTER XXXI.

THE SUN GONE DOWN.

'THERE, Miss Tandy what do you think of that?' said Jack when he had made an end of reading.

'I think it's very funny. Isn't it a little like Ossian? I never read the book, but I have seen occasional quotations from it.'

'It's all very well for you to be amused at it, but it's a different matter for me,' said Jack, sternly facing his editorial responsibilities. 'I have my reputation to consider, and my position in the journalistic world. I couldn't remain editor of a paper which contained stuff of that sort. What I've got to think of is whether I'll have the row now or next week.'

'And how do you divide the contingency?'

'Well, I may either at once return the manuscript to Fleyce, telling him I cannot insert it, or may take no notice of it, and let him make the discovery when the paper comes out on Thursday. That would be the ordinary way, as an editor is not bound to hold communication on the matter of rejected contributions even with his proprietor.'

'Isn't he, really? I have more and more admiration for your profession. Still, I think if I were in your place I should take the former course as being the more straightforward—I mean the more direct.'

'Thank you, Miss Tandy,' Jack replied with a sudden fervour that appeared to his companion altogether disproportionate to the service rendered. 'I shall take your advice, and as soon as I get back to the office will return the manuscript to Mr. Fleyce with a note explaining that I had already had arrange-

ments made for reporting the proceedings.
There will be a tremendous flare-up, and I
expect I'll have to go.'

'Go where?'

'Back to London, to see what I can pick
up there.   But for one thing I should be glad
to get out of this place, with its country ale and
its heavy people.   I feel I am losing myself,
spoiling my opportunities, which ought to lead
me to better things.'

' I am glad to hear you say that, Mr Bailey,'
said Napper, with kindly voice and look.   Any
aspiration after better things immediately
interested her, and she had always fancied there
was much good in this harum-scarum youth,
with his vast views, his large talk, and his
inconstant habits of industry.   'It is always a
bad sign for young men if they are satisfied
with what they are doing.   That sounds like a
moral maxim, and comes well from me, talking
to one who is so much cleverer and has seen so
much more of the world.'

'I hope you will say more of the same sort,' said Jack, with a well-defined notion that he would be content to be lectured all his life by this particular teacher.

'Thank you, I have not got a miscellaneous stock of wise sayings. It just occurred to me at the moment, and what I mean is that if you feel some disgust at these associations which you seem to group under the head of country ale, it is a good and hopeful sign.'

'There is one thing,' Jack remarked, beginning to talk a little rapidly, 'that has kept me here so long.'

'What is it?' said Napper, gently, with a bewitching intonation of sympathy in her voice.

She thought she knew only too well. She had heard something from Captain O'Brien of Jack's struggles in London, of his lonely and gallant fight with the hosts that bar the portal of journalism against unbefriended youth. Captain O'Brien had touched very little on the

Fleet Street bar episodes, but, wishing to interest the young lady in his *protégé*, had spoken at large on his straitened means and his constant struggle.

Napper thought of him now going back to the old battle-ground to begin over again the weary fight. Where would he sleep, and how would he eat, with such slender resources as he might have scraped together whilst living in the purple and fine linen of Gideon's service? When his store of ready money was exhausted, would he walk the streets all night, as Dr. Johnson had done, and would he finally choke himself in a ravenous encounter with an unaccustomed bone, as Savage did?

Any human sorrow touched the heart of Napper, making its way with swift incisive movement through her habitually self-possessed manner. When the sorrow came by self-sacrifice for conscience' sake, the feeling of sympathy was the quicker and the more tender. Jack, she knew, was pretty comfortably off at

Saxton. He had plenty of money for his modest needs, was popular in the town, and was autocratic at the office. After that struggle over the shirt sleeves and the pewter flagon, Gideon had retreated, and left the field in the possession of the young hero.

All this he was giving up for conscience' sake, because he did not think it consonant with his duties to find a place in the paper he edited for the windy rhetoric of his employer. It was like a non-juror going forth from home and all means of livelihood, preferring poverty to concessions which his conscience could not approve.

'What is it? Tell me everything,' she repeated, laying her hand on his arm, and looking into his face, with a sweet pleading that would have stormed the Torres Vedras of a stonier heart.

Alas! poor hapless Jack. It made a sudden and ignominious end of him, whose heart was not stony, and who had long surrendered its citadel to the unconscious besieger. With a quick movement he captured the little hand that lay trembling on his arm, and, carrying it to his lips, covered it with passionate kisses.

This, of course, was merely designed as the commencement of a familiar scene, enacted with minor alteration from the earliest ages. When Jacob met Rachel at the well and drew water for her, it was the beginning of a happy ending.

Thus, had things happened to turn out otherwise, it would have been with Jack Bailey. His kissing of Napper's glove was, in his own mind, the counterpart of Jacob's drawing the water for Rachel. Doubtless Rachel, looking shyly interested in the unwonted action of the stranger, flashed from soft black eyes the signal that all was well, and that if Jacob had anything more to say or do tending in kindly directions he might go on. Indeed he did, for we read that ' Jacob kissed Rachel,' a further attention which she demurely accepted.

Napper's eyes flashed, but not quite after the fashion we have imagined Rachel's to shine. Jack saw the fire and began to think there was a mistake somewhere. But he didn't go any further in his self-abasement than to suppose he had been a little hasty, and had omitted certain preliminaries, gratifying to maidenly reserve, and proper to be observed before the young man seizes the maiden's hand, and proceeds to act towards it much after the manner that Napper, a moment earlier, had been picturing to herself Savage wrestling with the fatally delayed bone.

'There, Napper darling,' said Jack, dropping her hand, but not lowering his glance from the crimson face and flashing eyes that blazed in heart-crushing indignation before him. 'You know now what I mean.'

'I do *not* know what you mean, Mr.

Bailey,' cried Napper, retreating beyond arm's length of the youth. 'But if you mean to be rude I am exceedingly sorry for it, and, if you please, will leave you here.'

She had turned with a quick movement, and was off in the direction of town before Jack had quite realised the force of her words. Once spoken, their meaning was only too clear, and resistance could not long be maintained even by the pitiful desperate hope Jack spoke to his heart, that he might be mistaken, and that things were not so bad as they looked. With some girls all this might be a flush of outraged modesty, not necessarily simulated.

Jack had certainly been a little abrupt. Suddenly to drop from the altitude of literary disquisition to kissing a girl's hand was a long way.

When he came to look at matters in the chilled mood that followed on the thunder of his attack and the lightning of her repulse, he admitted he had been a little hasty. If Napper's mind had been prepared for such an outburst by long meditation, as his own had been, it would have been a different thing. Five minutes ago—and what a boundless space of time five minutes was!—Jack had not taken these circumstances into account. He was always thinking of Napper. Night or day the thought of her did not leave his mind, and she would have been at least pleased to know how much the shrine was purified by this constant presence. What was familiar to Jack must, he had anxiously come to think, be known also to Napper.

Interpreting her thoughts and actions by his own it was small wonder that, when he had led up to the critical point and she had responded with that gentle touch on his arm, and that tender glance through dew-dimmed eyes, he should have fallen headlong into the pit. It was, if poor Jack had only known it, a natural love for mankind that moved Napper, and that is a sadly different thing from love for a particular man. Jack had made a mistake, an irremediable mistake, he felt certain. But if Napper was lost to him, indeed had never been found by him, he must not entirely forfeit her good opinion and let her leave him with the shock of this rude attack unmitigated.

She had not been gone three minutes before these reflections and a thousand others had passed through the mind of Jack. She was beginning to descend the path which led over the Downs into the town, with Knut scampering round her.

Happy, enviable Knut! who lived daily in her presence, and was not unfrequently fondled under the very eyes of hapless men.

Jack looked with blurred eyes over the Downs. Beyond the grassy slope spread the blue sea with a ship going home under full sail, and between him and the sea this straight lithe figure walking steadily forward, and swiftly disappearing. Poor, miserable, hopeless Jack! It seemed as if the sun were going down behind the horizon, and that thereafter for all time there would be only black night for him, with peradventure such mournful light as might come from the clouds of memory, brooding above the setting sun and dwelling in heaven half the night.

He might for ever keep with him the memory of Napper's beauty, of her purity of mind and thought, of her high disdain of all that was mean and ignoble, of her quick sympathy with all that was good, and of her tender loving-kindness even with some that was bad.

In particular Jack felt an insane delight in the knowledge that he had called her 'darling' within her hearing. It was no new term in this application. But hitherto it was only to himself that Jack, with his heart full of love, had murmured the word. Now he had spoken it out, and, in some odd illogical way, it seemed to him to give him a possession in her.

All this was sorrowful; but Jack felt that

he had this advantage over the ordinary arrangements of nature, that if his sun was truly sinking over the horizon he might with no great effort overtake it, and at least temporarily keep it company. Things were very bad, but it would have been worse if, even for an hour, he left Napper in the mood he had seen her in when she turned her proud face from him.

Napper presently heard his rapid footsteps behind her, and when they came quite close she stopped and confronted him. There was no notion in her mind of running away. She had turned and walked off on the first impulse of the annoyance and insult she had suffered. But she felt perfectly capable of taking care of herself, and when she heard Jack following she stopped and looked round precisely as she would have done had she been walking alone in ordinary circumstances, and heard some one hurrying up behind her.

'Miss Tandy,' said Jack, taking off his hat

and standing bareheaded, 'I wish to beg your pardon. I have in the most abominable manner spoiled your walk, and as I may not see you again I just wished to say this, and to hope that you will forgive me, and will try and think no more of what has passed to-day. I have made a fool of myself, a recollection that will be hard enough for me to bear; but what I said, or rather what I did, was on a sudden impulse, and altogether under a misapprehension. I hope you will say you will forgive me, and will try and believe that I at least meant honestly and well.'

'I do believe it, Mr. Bailey,' Napper said, holding out her hand without the slightest apprehension of danger of its undergoing a repetition of former sufferance. 'I do believe it, and I am very sorry.'

Jack took the hand, and behaved exceedingly well. He didn't even return the warm pressure which Napper, in her inexperience, and having a habitude of submitting to impulses, had given to his. He touched it respectfully and released it gently.

Napper's self-possession, under what were certainly embarrassing circumstances, helped him to regain his. The instincts of a gentleman, which underlay a manner somewhat maimed by the boisterous companionship of Fleet Street, came out on this critical occasion, and he bore himself with a grave and courtly dignity that Napper noted as something quite new.

'Then, since I am forgiven, Miss Tandy,' he said, still remaining uncovered, 'I shall venture to ask a favour. When we met I was going into town, and you were going out for your morning walk. Will you permit me to go my way whilst you give Knut that run which he is so anxious for?'

'Certainly, Mr. Bailey. I think I should like to have my walk. Good morning.'

'Good-bye,' said Jack, with graceful courtesy and a gallant effort not to seem sad.

So Napper went her way inland, Knut frisking about in great joy at the new turn affairs had taken, whilst Jack, turning his face to the sea, walked rapidly into the town, and, shutting himself up in his editorial sanctorum, remained for a quarter of an hour in a state of limp and abject misery, a relapse from the high condition into which he had been nerved by the contemplation of Napper's excellence and his own unworthiness.

Then he rose, despatched the printers' boy for a pint of stout, which being brought in a pewter measure, he sat down to his desk, took off his coat, lit his pipe, and proceeded to indite a few lines to his esteemed proprietor.

CHAPTER XXXII.

BREAKING IT GENTLY.

THE humble house in Camden Town, to which Mr. Dumfy had once made touching reference when in conversation with Gideon, will be found in the Directory as No. 15 Pelton Street. Pelton Street is some thirty houses long, all two stories high, all with little gardens in front inclosed by iron railings, in various conditions ranging from dilapidation to trimness, and nearly all eminently respectable in look.

Mr. Dumfy's neighbours were on the whole above him in the social scale, or at least in the money scale. The houses were rented at thirty pounds a year, which, when you come to add rates, represented a fact prohibitory to Mr. Dumfy's tenancy. But the house had been taken with a view to an arrangement by which a lodger or lodgers should pay the rent. There was a front parlour and two bedrooms at the disposal of 'two gentlemen (brothers or otherwise) engaged in the City during the day. Cleanliness given and required.'

This stipulation in the Dumfy advertisement is perhaps accountable for its frequent appearance in the daily newspapers. Cleanliness is admitted on high authority to hold the next place to godliness. But Mr. Waffle was sometimes disturbed by a suspicion that in the case of Mrs. Dumfy the relative positions were reversed.

'If Sister Dumfy thought of people's immortal souls as much as she thinks of the sole that perisheth, and certainly is prone to bring mud into the apartment, it would be well.'

This sardonic remark was wrung from the pastor, on an occasion when, paying a visit of consolation and comfort, he had been vigorously reproached by Mrs. Dumfy for disregarding

the mat at the door and tainting the spotless
floor of the kitchen.

Mrs. Dumfy was always dusting, or wash-
ing, or polishing, so that her house became a
somewhat painful model of cleanliness.

' You might eat your dinner off my kitchen
floor,' she was accustomed to say with worldly
pride, and a total disregard of the circumstance that no one in their senses would desire
to have the principal meal of the day so
served.

Her habits were somewhat aggressive, it
must be admitted, and greatly militated against
the lodging business. The locality was convenient enough for young men, whether
brothers or otherwise, who spent their day in
the City. A fair proportion were willing to
submit to the requirements of cleanliness ; but
Mrs. Dumfy was too exacting, and relations
entered upon with some promise of a favourable conclusion were often abruptly closed
either by the lodger stamping out of the house

with the agonised declaration that he 'could stand this no longer,' or by the appearance of Mrs. Dumfy at the door, reproachfully holding on a shovel the last clod of earth which, brought indoors, had broken the back of her patience. With the clod came the request that the young gentlemen would 'suit themselves elsewhere.'

On the Monday morning following the Sunday, when we saw the good lady placidly seated in the pew at Rehoboth, she was having what she called a 'turn out.' This was a matter of such frequent occurrence as scarcely to call for remark here, save that there was just now the exceptional occasion that on the previous Saturday two young gentlemen from the City, who had proved undesirable tenants, had departed, and now Mrs. Dumfy was, as she said, 'tidying up.'

If the young gentlemen from the City had been carried out in coffins, having died of small-pox, cholera, or other malignant disease, Mrs.

Dumfy's procedure could hardly have been more exhaustive. All the windows were opened to their utmost capacity. The beds were turned down, the carpets were up, a vigorous sweeping had been going on since day-break, and two gentlemen who stood at the door knocking were detained for some time by the circumstance that at the moment of their arrival Mrs. Dumfy was in the back-yard struggling violently with a carpet from which, with the assistance of the greengrocer's boy, she was vainly endeavouring to extract some proof of dust.

It was a part of Mrs. Dumfy's pleasure that she did all the work of the house herself. ' To have a slatternly servant,' as she said, ' making dirt all over the place she never would.' She had once tried a compromise in the person of a charwoman, but had never repeated the experiment.

A little wiry woman, it seemed as if nearly every morsel of flesh had been dusted or scoured off her. She looked frail, but was certainly strong enough to do what lay to her hand, and should have brought a blush of shame to the brow of the greengrocer's boy by comparison of the vigorous way in which she dealt with the carpet and the deprecatory manner in which he handled it.

This youth was a constant terror to her whilst he remained in the neighbourhood of the premises. Of course he never entered the house, being admitted by the door of the back-yard, by which portal he also departed on the receipt of fourpence. But Mrs. Dumfy was always haunted by the suspicion that he cherished dark designs, and sometimes when Mr. Dumfy was away she awoke in the dead of the night in cold perspiration, having dreamed that the greengrocer's boy had got in, walked all over the house with his boots on, and had laid himself at full length on the chintz-covered sofa in the parlour.

One of the two gentlemen at the front

door, bringing his eye to the level of the key-hole, perceived through the narrow corridor Mrs. Dumfy at the other end, engaged with the greengrocer's boy. Satisfied with this evidence that there was some one at home, and that there would presently be a response at the front door, they possessed their souls in patience and occupied the interval in glancing up and down the street, from many windows of which they were already the object of regard.

The parlour window, being on the level of the street, was closed lest peradventure dust might enter, disturbed by passing feet. In the window was a card announcing 'Apartments.' Perhaps the two callers were City gentlemen (brothers or otherwise) seeking apartments, and prepared on their part to meet reasonable requirements in the matter of cleanliness.

They certainly did not look like the ordinary type of City gentlemen. One was tall and thin, with a pale cadaverous face in which gleamed two large black eyes, and whose black hair fell at greater length over his shoulders than is the habit in the City. The other was short and stout, with a ruddy face, inclined to be blotchy, and prominent eyes of the gooseberry order. He was much more like a City man, insomuch that he had a brisk business air, and regarded every passer-by with curious intent, as if he were considering whether the errand he had at heart would be promoted by addressing him.

'Gracious me! Brother Waffle and Brother Selth,' said Mrs. Dumfy, when a fresh assault on the knocker succeeded in attracting her attention. 'Who'd ha' thought o' seeing you a Monday morning and with the house all up and not a mat down anywhere. Perhaps you won't mind me asking you in to-day as you wouldn't be very comfortable.'

'We've come to speak to you, Sister Dumfy, on a little matter that I fear will necessitate our intruding on your household convenience.'

'Yes, Sister Dumfy,' chimed in Brother

Selth, who had cast over his accustomed briskness of manner a sort of pall of cotton-velvet, ' we've a little word to say about a matter of great moment.'

' Oh dear ! oh dear ! ' wailed Mrs. Dumfy, who was not wont to control her feelings on these occasions; ' then please to scrape your boots, and don't come in till I fetch a mat.'

Whereupon she turned off and presently re-appeared with a door mat, anxiously watching the brethren as they made diligent use of it. Brother Selth was so vigorous in his performance as to overstep the mark, and to extract from Mrs. Dumfy a despairing groan at the prospect of the mud he was kicking out over the oilcloth, only that morning washed and bees-waxed.

' Sister Dumfy,' said the Rev. Mr. Waffle, when the party were seated in the little parlour, ' something has happened in our little community, and Brother Selth and me, talking it over, came to the conclusion it was our duty to come and break it gently to you.'

'You haven't heard anything?' said Brother Selth, eagerly, fearful lest they might have been forestalled.

'No,' replied Mrs. Dumfy, with a scared look, peering round her with a dim apprehension that a bucket of water had been kicked over somewhere. 'I haven't been out this morning, and there's been no one near the place except that greengrocer's boy, and he hasn't been in the house to my knowledge, though no one can say what he'd do if my back was turned for a moment.'

'Ah!' said Mr. Selth, drawing in a deep breath of satisfaction, and rubbing his knees with a large content.

'Yes,' Mr. Waffle continued, raising his eyes to the ceiling, 'it is a lamentable occurrence. The like of it has never before disturbed the peace of Rehoboth.'

'Dear me!' said Mrs. Dumfy, with quick

sympathy. 'Don't tell me that horrid water pipe's bust again and messed the whole place about.'

'Worse than that,' groaned Brother Selth.

'Much worse,' echoed Brother Waffle. 'A pipe can be mended, and the flow of liquid stopped! but there is some things as can't never be mended once they're broke. When the silvery cord is snapped and the golden bowl a broken, you can't do nothing to set *them* right again.'

'I was once,' said Brother Selth, who, however mournful might have been the errand to which he attuned his voice, seemed to be thoroughly enjoying himself, 'I was once, in the days of sin, at a theayter, and remember one of the adycamps coming in to the general —the Earl of Essex, I think he was—and he says, "My lord, the dook's wownded." "What, wownded?" says the earl. "Ay, wownded," says the adycamp. "Not mortially wownded?"

says the earl. " Ay, mor-ti-al-ly wownded," says the adycamp." '

The last line Brother Selth gave with great dramatic force, making much of the syllables in mortally, and placing his hands over his eyes and turning away his head as if he could not bear contemplation of the scene conjured up.

Mrs. Dumfy looked from one to the other with startled gaze.

'What d'ye mean, Brother Waffle and Brother Selth?' she said sharply. ' If there's anything happened at the chapel that I oughter know, just out with it, and don't be making these mysteries.'

' I don't myself quite follow Brother Selth,' said Mr. Waffle, a little coldly.

'It's a hallegory, Brother,' Mr. Selth explained, a little snappishly, feeling confident that, as compared with the pastor's procedure, his own notion of breaking the news was much more subtle and effective.

'Oh, if it's an allegory, very well; but, you see, Sister Dumfy is a little agitated, and doesn't quite follow it.'

'No, that I don't,' said Mrs. Dumfy, querulously, with her hand at her heart. 'I don't know what you are going to break, but the fall cannot be much worse than what you're saying and looking now.'

'Ah!' sighed Brother Selth, continuing the gentle rubbing of his knees, and gazing round at the furniture with a professionally sympathising look, as if he were an undertaker, and had come to measure the various articles for coffins.

It was Brother Waffle's salaried business to talk, and, if he thought he could do it better, Brother Selth was not going to cross him.

'Be calm, good Sister Dumfy, and prepare yourself for a blow that falls on all of us sooner or later. But the wounded back maketh a contrite heart.'

Mrs. Dumfy sat rigidly upright, looking from one to the other of her visitors. They were evidently very much in earnest, and there had come home to her a swift inspiration of the nature of their news. This unwonted call, these sad looks, this talk of the broken bowl and the mortal wound, could mean only one thing. Mr. Dumfy had not always been a good husband to her. But now there came upon her a sudden sinking of the heart, a whirring noise in the head, and the thought that she should never see him again.

'You've not heard anything from Brother Dumfy this morning?' Mr. Waffle asked, whilst Brother Selth, with his head on one side, and his gooseberry eyes growing increasingly goggled, heaved another sigh.

'No, I've not; have you?' Mrs. Dumfy asked, in the same sharp tone.

'In the midst of life we are in death,' Brother Selth cut in, bursting with desire to be the first to convey the news, and yet feeling the necessity of yielding something to Mr. Waffle's clerical position. ' Here to-day and gone to-morrow. Life's worse, Sister Dumfy, even than last year's cut in trousers. That may come up again, but when once you're dead you're gone, and your place knows you no more.'

Mrs. Dumfy lifted up her voice and wept long before Brother Selth had come to the conclusion of this homily, which he pursued with the greater unction as he watched its effect.

' What is it, Brother Waffle ? ' she said through her sobs, instinctively turning away from the blotched face, gooseberry eyes, and oily head of hair on her right.

' It's a railway accident,' said Mr. Waffle, who, being of a finer tissue than Brother Selth, had not been unconscious of a feeling of dis-gust, as he watched that individual, who, with his hands crossed over his well-rounded con-tour, was ogling the ceiling in a manner apparently understood by himself as expressive of the deepest sympathy, and meanwhile sighing like a seal. 'A railway accident, my sister; and we were not altogether without expectation that the Lord had watched over his sheep from our little fold, and that something might have happened to prevent his going by that particular train. We just did look to find him here, but very faintly.'

'Very!' said Brother Selth, determined not to be hustled out of the conversation.

'I've never seed nor heard anything of him,' Mrs. Dumfy wailed, 'since he was settin' under the pulpit last night, and then went to the vestry for his bag. He told me at tea-time he was going from Charing Cross at eight o'clock, and wouldn't be home for a fortnight owing to the Election coming on. Oh dear, dear, dear! I felt sure something was wrong when I opened the door and seed Brother Selth with his hat on, and this a Monday.'

'A very dreadful business,' said Mr. Waffle.

' Afore coming here we telegraphed to Saxton to know if 'he had arrived, but he had not been seen or heard of there.'

They spoke always of ' he ' and ' him,' forgetful that Mr. Dumfy's name had not yet been mentioned.

' And then we talked the matter over,' Brother Selth said, shooting in again. ' I saw it in the paper this morning, and leaving the shop and the customers by, I went over to Brother Waffle's. We knowed he'd ha' gone down in that train, and I says to Brother Waffle, " If he's not arrived safe he's in it, so we'll telegraph ; " and telegraph we did, getting it all in for a shillin', and there's the answer from Mr. Landy.'

Brother Selth produced the telegram, and having first spread it out on his knee as if it was a sample of trousering, handed it to the widow. It was from Mr. Tandy, ' Mr. Landy ' being a mere trifling with the orthography of proper names not uncommon in telegraphic communications. The purport of the message was clear enough.

'*Your message passed on to me. Dumfy did not arrive last night, nor is anything known of him this morning*'

Mrs. Dumfy felt that this was her husband's death warrant, and she broke into fresh wailing that found the heart of Mr. Waffle behind its. encrustation of Rehobothism.

'I've got the paper here, if you'd like to see the particulars,' said Brother Selth, laboriously tugging in his tail pockets.

'No, no,' said Brother Waffle, quickly holding up his hand to guard the broken-down woman from this fresh anguish. 'Sister Dumfy won't care to see that now. But I think we must go down to the scene and identify our dear departed. Perhaps, Brother Selth, your business avocations would make it inconvenient for you to accompany us.'

'Yes, that's true,' said Brother Selth, casting anew his dismal glance upon the ceiling, and meanwhile rapidly turning over in his mind the circumstance that on these painful occasions the railway companies are only too liberal in their facilities for the gratuitous movement of friends of the victims of disaster. He would certainly get a railway journey free, and would have the further enjoyment of that odd luxury which some kind people find in the company of mourners, and in an atmosphere exhilarated by calamity. 'There'll be a nice difference in the takings to-day, I know ; but dooty's dooty, friendship's friendship, and brotherhood is not to be a broken reed that crumbles up just when you want to lean upon it. I'll go with our sister and brother here and visit the silent tomb.'

So it was settled, and the three went down the line by which less than twenty-four hours earlier Mr. Dumfy had travelled, with his head full of schemes for additional contributions from petty cash, and by which a little later Gideon had gone, desperate and despairing.

Before drawing down the blind and shutting up the house Mrs. Dumfy had put on a black dress, and gone rooting about in old boxes for a bit of black crape wherewith to deck her green widowhood. She found on the spot many sisters in sorrow, for the catastrophe had claimed a host of victims. If she had been in the mood for observing, she would have noticed that whilst the wealthier had come to the scene in such attire as the news had found them in, women of the poorer class, like herself, had been punctilious in putting on whatever black they possessed, and in hastily fitting on to their bonnets forlorn bits of crape.

In all there were fifteen parcels made up, and laid out in the station room, whither they had been carried. It was a piteous scene, and the air was full of lamentation, for a fresh sorrow had been added to the anguish of the bereaved. Who could tell, looking on these charred and blackened faces, which had been the husband, the wife, the son, though to know this was all the world to the man or the woman who, with various show of sorrow—some loudly weeping, others tearless and silent, looking out on the bloomless world with stony faces—had come to claim their dead.

Even to the physical sense, the atmosphere of the charnel house was sickening. But Brother Selth thoroughly enjoyed himself. There was nothing of the vulture about him, and he was even unfeignedly sorry that Sister Dumfy and the rest should be sad. But into his narrow life there rarely came flashes of excitement. If one had now fallen upon him, and if as a friend of one of the victims he was treated with distinguished consideration by the railway officials, who can blame him if he were inclined to make the most of his opportunity, or that he bustled hither and thither with a well-meant heartiness that involuntarily suggested to the able-bodied mourner the fierce delight that would underlay the exercise of choking him?

It was he who, going hither and thither, careful that no germ of emotion should be lost, came upon conclusive evidence of poor Dumfy's doom. In the station-master's office were spread out a collection of *débris* from the fire, charred tin trunks, bits of burned portmanteaus, singed travelling rugs, and other relics of the impedimenta of the crowd of railway passengers. Amongst these, partly mutilated, wholly discoloured, but clearly recognisable, was the metal handle of Mr. Dumfy's umbrella. The old gingham had melted like a snowflake on a river. The antiquated thick whalebone ribs had opened for the last time, and the stick was in ashes. But here was the sturdy metal knob, all that was left of Brother Dumfy—all but the parcel in the adjoining room, though which parcel was he poor lean little Mrs. Dumfy felt with bitter anguish could not be told.

There was no mistaking the umbrella handle, and Mrs. Dumfy, going back with red eyes to her lonely home, reproached herself for the many times she had fallen upon her husband and berated him for alleged delinquencies at the door-mat.

'If he'd only come back to-night,' she moaned as she threw herself on the chair in the fireless kitchen and cast her apron over her face, ' he might step over all the mats, and walk through the house in the muddiest boots he could make through Tottenham Court Road.'

END OF THE SECOND VOLUME.

LONDON : PRINTED BY
SPOTTISWOODE AND CO., NEW-STREET SQUARE
AND PARLIAMENT STREET

www.ingramcontent.com/pod-product-compliance
Lightning Source LLC
Chambersburg PA
CBHW020926120726
47905CB00008B/2396